For Nancy,
Savor the good memories

Annabelle and the Sandhog

Ray Paul

ISBN: 1492866571
ISBN 13: 9781492866572

SANDHOG is the slang term given to urban miners, construction workers who work underground on a variety of excavation projects in major cities. Generally these projects involve tunneling, caisson excavation or some other type of underground construction. The miners work with a variety of equipment from tunnel boring machines to using dynamite to blast a path for the project they are building. The term SANDHOG is an American colloquialism.

Over the past one hundred years this relatively small group of men have performed the majority of underground work in cities like New York, Baltimore and Chicago. In their unseen world of rock, sand and earth, these men struggle with the forces of nature and ultimately their own life and death. Without question, SANDHOGS are a brotherhood of men who share extremely hard work and constant danger.

The men who have worked in this dangerous occupation have generally been the under-educated new arrivals to the American shores who were attracted to the higher paying but more dangerous jobs often shunned by earlier arrivals. Many men of Irish descent became SANDHOGS as did black men from the Caribbean islands and rural areas of the United States. While Sandhogging has been a stepping stone for many men, it is often a tradition that is passed down through generations of families; since mining projects span decades, it is not uncommon to find multi-generations of families working together on the same job.

SANDHOGS go where no man has ever gone before.

DEDICATION

For Jo Marie, my partner in marriage for 55 years, and my partner in writing
all six of my published books.

O'Malley
Family Tree

John O'Malley (8/12/1882–   )
m. Florence Ferland (4/17/1885–   )

|

Mike O'Malley (11/7/1907–   )
m. Sara Miller (12/9/1909–   )

|

Tim O'Malley (2/25/1936–   )
m. Claire Sheridan (6/15/1936–   )

Michael (9/18/1959–   )   Marie (2/2/1965–8/13/1970)

Chapter 1

JOHN O'MALLEY

The white one is making my bed this morning. She's the one who's snippy half the time and totally pissed off the rest. Even though my damn macular degeneration won't let me see much of anything these days, just blurry images, I know when she's around. I can sense her testiness the minute she marches through the door. I feel the chill that follows her into the room like a dense fog rolling off the Atlantic on the coast of Maine where I grew up. The temperature drops twenty degrees when she passes my wheelchair. She doesn't have to say anything. Good thing, because she usually doesn't. I just know it's her because I can feel her presence and hear her sometimes, even smell her although about all I can make out of her facial features is she isn't black like Annabelle.

I always could sense things even though I may not have always used good sense. That's why I'm still around at ninety-two, I suppose. If I hadn't been able to know what was happening around me, I'd have died accidentally or someone would have done me in long before I was forty. While that might make a good story for my grandson Tim's tape recorder, I don't feel much like talking right now with the pissy one around. Too bad I didn't think of that story yesterday, because that was a good day. Annabelle made my bed. Actually, every day is a pretty good day, except the days Annabelle comes around are better. She has a big butt, and she's such a good egg. And, she likes me. How can I tell? I don't know, I just sense she does. It certainly has nothing to do with my sweet-talking her. Everything I try to say is so jumbled up since my last stroke a year ago, she'd never be able to tell if I was sweet talking her or not. Still, she knows I like her, too. How do I know she knows? Hell, I guess I really don't know except...except, I just know she does.

Yesterday, I was sitting in my wheelchair, daydreaming, when she came in to make my bed. Since I like being near her, I kind of wheel around after her, and because I'm closer when I do that, she seems to work slower and stay longer. What is it Tim says? "It works for me."

Anyway, at one point I'm pretty close to her, and she's bending over, and even with my poor eyesight I spot her large behind. Suddenly the Devil in me takes control of my hand and gently slaps her fanny.

At first there isn't much of a reaction. Not a giggle or a surprised yelp or a "Why, I do declare John O'Malley! You're a might frisky this morning." But, there's just silence. I can imagine if it had been the white woman's butt, she'd have screamed for the orderly, and I'd have been tossed out of Highland Manor and left in the street to die before I had a chance to explain myself–which of course, I couldn't because my speech is all garbled and anyway the Devil made me do it.

All she says is, "Why did you do that, Mr. O'Malley?" Since I trust my hearing, and there's amusement in her voice, I don't get all panicky because I'm sure she doesn't really need an explanation or even want one. She knows a harmless pat on the fanny is about the only manly thing I can muster up these days. I wheel back to give her more space and say, "Cuseywatato." I know it comes out garbled and is probably incomprehensible to her, but I hear her chuckle, and she doesn't rush to move away even though she's finished with her tucking and smoothing.

Finally, she straightens and pushes my chair slightly so she can move to the window and pull up the Venetian blinds. The light glares off my cataracts. Still, I see her silhouette against the sun-drenched pane, or imagine I do. I hear the window squeak open. A soft breeze reaches me, and I smell apple blossoms. At first I'm perplexed. Why would there be apple trees outside my window in this sterile jail for oldsters, but the smell is unmistakable. Maybe it's all imaginary, but I do know the smell of apple blossoms, and I do know it's May and while surprising, the builder could have left some old apple trees on the grounds when he built the place. I would have in my day.

A shadow crosses my face, and I feel her lips briefly brush my forehead.

"Is there anything else I can do for you, Mr. O'Malley? Maybe push you to the window? It's a beautiful spring day. A day that would turn any young man's fancy to love."

"Why did you kiss me?" I say, although I'm sure she doesn't understand my words. Hell, I just said them, and I don't understand them. How could she? Damn, it's so frustrating not being able to talk to her.

Gently, she places a soothing hand on my shoulder and mimicking my earlier garble, says, "Because I wanted to." She then pushes me toward the window, kisses my forehead again and silently slips through the doorway.

When she leaves, I feel the tears well up in my eyes. I don't disturb them, choosing instead to savor them. God, it feels good to know she understands me.

It seems like months since my son, Mike, has come to Highland Manor to see me, so before she left for the day I asked Annabelle about it. She thought for a moment, and said it might be more like two weeks. I think she's wrong, because it seems like two months, but who am I to argue with a young woman who has her wits about her. When it comes to arguments with women, I haven't won one since the day I married Flo seventy some years ago.

Still, I wonder what's keeping my son away. It's not like him to stick me here in Highland Manor and not visit me. Since he's the one who pays the bills to keep me penned up in this place, you'd think he'd want to check up on his investment. Actually, for a few years after Flo and I pulled up stakes in Michigan and moved in with Mike and his wife, Sara, I saw him about every day. That was hard, too, on all of us, I'm sure. Too much closeness can be just as bad as too much loneliness. No matter how much you might love your kid or him you, four headstrong adults with varying needs and ways of doing things crammed together in a single-family home puts a strain on everyone.

We solved that problem the hard way. Flo died of a heart attack, I had my second stroke and Sara's dementia was already so bad, Mike had to have a woman come in every day to care for her. Can you imagine being cooped up all day with that poor mindless creature and her caretaker while I'm in grief and trying to learn to speak again with the therapist Mike hired for me? The whole set-up drove me nuts. I could only think of two remedies, die or get me out of there. When God didn't provide an out, Mike came through and placed me in Highland Manor.

What a difference. Even though I would like to see Mike more, I do enjoy seeing Tim and telling stories to his machine. Mostly, though, as the kids say, I like "hanging out" with Annabelle.

Chapter 2

TIM O'MALLEY

She was only five and a half, a joyous curly-haired bundle of affection. One day in August of 1970 when we were vacationing on a lake near Boyne Falls, Michigan, she was playing at the water's edge with the other little kids. The next day she was on a ventilator fighting a losing battle for her life.

Spinal meningitis the doctor said. That night they found a room for my wife and me at the hospital so we could be near her when she woke up. Marie never did. After a couple of days, tests confirmed her brain waves were flat, so the pediatrician in that nightmare shut off the ventilator. Moments later, two persons died. Little Marie went to heaven, and I've been tromping through hell ever since.

I've been told hundreds of times by doctors and others that these tragedies just happen, and there was nothing my wife, Claire, nor I could have done to save her. But, they don't know the whole story. Only Claire and I know the truth. In the early afternoon a few days before she died, little Marie complained to my wife about an earache. Claire also noticed she had developed a drippy nose. Because we were far from our home in Illinois and our usual pediatrician, we decided to play it safe. So, in mid-afternoon we packed Marie into the car and drove the twenty-some miles to the minuscule clinic attached to the hospital in the small tourist town. As luck would have it, the hospital's only pediatrician didn't work that day, so we were ushered into the office of a general practitioner. I'll never forget the guy. Dr. Smithson was a slightly built man in his fifties who displayed his lack of conviction by talking in a near-whisper. To further shake our confidence in his diagnostic skills, he spent the whole time he was checking Marie's ears, nose and throat apologizing for the pediatrician's absence.

"It's probably just a bug she's picked up," he said. "I wouldn't want to prescribe any medicine for fear of masking the symptoms. If she's feeling worse in the morning, bring her back when Dr. Wainwright is here." Then, he guided her back to Claire with the reassuring words, "I'm sure it's nothing serious."

On the ride home Marie was hopping around the back seat, gazing out the window and generally confirming the doctor's diagnosis. We readily agreed it had been better to be safe than sorry. Upon arriving back at the rental cottage about five, Claire fed her some leftover soup and half of a cheese sandwich which she hardly touched. Afterwards, she played quietly for awhile. Around seven, Marie willingly put on her pajamas and let her mom tuck her in with a bedtime story.

Putting worry aside, I prepared for an evening of fishing on the lake. I made myself a sandwich, wrapped it in a paper napkin and stuck it into a plastic bag. I also stuffed a Budweiser into each pocket of my fishing pants and wrapped another in my rain poncho. Kissing Claire, I headed for the pier. After stepping down into the aluminum boat, I cranked up the motor and pulled away from the dock. Free of any anxiety about my daughter's health, I looked forward to trying some of my favorite spots on the lake and catching a few walleyes to feed the family.

About ten, I returned to the dock with three empty beer cans and four two-pound keepers in the live-well. I had just brought the fish into the screened-in, fish-cleaning shanty when our son, Michael, raced down the hill and yelled through the screen, "Something's happened to Marie. Mom wants you to come right away."

I glanced at the fish flopping on the counter and vowed to clean them immediately after I looked into whatever crisis was brewing. Together Michael and I raced up the slope to the cabin. Once inside, I encountered Claire holding our daughter in her arms. I gasped. Marie was convulsing.

"Where have you been," Claire screamed. "She just started this, and I'm scared to death."

Rather than try to defend myself, I took Marie from her and held her gently against my chest. "Grab the car keys," I whispered, thinking my voice might startle her. "We're going back to the hospital. You drive. I'll ride in the back seat and hold her."

"What about me?" Michael asked.

"You can either sleep in your bed or go next door and ask the Nelsons to find a place for you over there. You're almost twelve for gosh sakes. We've got to go. Now!" I saw the confusion in his eyes, but I didn't respond. Claire was already waiting in the car.

Pulling up to the Emergency Room entrance, we raced through the door with Marie in my arms and Claire following close behind. A lone nurse rose from behind a desk and immediately called the pediatrician, the same doctor we had attempted to see earlier in the afternoon. After a cursory look at Marie who was still convulsing in my arms, the doctor snarled, "How long has she been like this? You have a very sick child." He shook his head. "Why didn't you bring her in sooner?"

Before we could defend ourselves or blame the guy who had seen our daughter six hours earlier, the doctor had handed Marie off to a nurse with whispered instructions. "It looks like an advanced case of meningitis," he said with a sense of dread in his voice. "We'll run some tests to be sure and do what we can."

His diagnosis was right. It was a fulminating case of bacterial spinal meningitis. Marie never opened her eyes again. After several days on a ventilator, it was turned off and life ended for us as well. We spent the remainder of our family vacation making arrangements for her funeral back in Illinois. Then, the following morning we gathered our belongings, packed Michael into the back seat and drove four hundred miles in silence. While I didn't realize it back in 1971, I was about to begin a period of self-loathing and guilt for my role in her death. Four years later, rightly or wrongly, I'm still blaming myself for trading what turned out to be an evening on the lake and four flopping fish for my young daughter's life.

Chapter 3

TIM O'MALLEY

In the early 1960's I bought a big, clunky Ampex magnetic reel tape recorder, ostensibly to capture our son Michael's earliest words and preserve them for posterity. To make full use of the machine, I also provided background to his utterances with tunes from my short, closet folk singing and guitar playing career. In reality, I played and sang for my own amazement, but I do have it all on tape should the rest of the world ever care to listen.

Like so many things that temporarily brought excitement into my life, like my baseball hat and postage stamp collections, once the novelty of taping wore off, I found a place for the recorder in a hard to reach spot on a high shelf in the spare bedroom closet and let it collect dust.

In 1971 after Marie had died, my paternal grandparents, John and Florence O'Malley, broke up their household in Montague, Michigan and moved in with my parents, Mike and Sara O'Malley, in Rockford, Illinois. Now, as anyone who has ever been around my grandfather knows, he has a lifetime of stories in his head, and he loves telling them to any and all willing listeners–especially his grandson.

After listening to a few dozen examples in the weeks that followed their arrival, I found the gloom that had surrounded me since Marie's death lifting slightly. I also remembered the old recorder, so I dusted it off and made sure it still worked. Then, I hauled it to my parents' home and plugged it into a wall socket in the spare bedroom where my grandparents had settled in. After showing my grandfather how the machine worked, which wasn't easy because of his advanced age and seriously impaired vision from macular degeneration, I handed him the small microphone and said, "Grandpa, please record any story you remember from your life, and I'll type each one up and edit it. Then, I'll put them together and make a book. We'll call it *The Diary of a Sandhog.*"

He looked up at me and grinned. "You'd do that for me?"

"I'll do that for you, me and everyone who reads it. You've had quite a life."

"I'd live it over if I could." Then, taking the microphone from me and touching various parts of the recorder, he said, "I don't see too well. Show me again how this thing works."

I took his hand and made him feel each switch, dial and button as I gave him a verbal rundown of the total operation. A few days later he dictated his first story and for the next few months kept me busy typing up his recollections. I thought the stories would never stop. And, frankly, I hoped they wouldn't, because getting involved in his life when I wasn't at work gave me a focus and distracted me somewhat from my mourning.

Then, in a period of months, my grandmother died suddenly, my mother's forgetfulness was diagnosed as dementia and grandpa had a small stroke. For awhile my dad tried to get by with a caretaker coming to the house every day, until finally he had no other choice than to place my mother into an assisted living facility. Then grandpa had a second stroke. Following his release from the hospital, he moved to the nursing home where he resides today. Not to be outdone, I sunk into another deep depression.

You'd think with his own suffering and all the misery going on around him, grandpa would just pack it in. But, Grandpa O'Malley is not a typical guy in his nineties. He lives for the moment. He wisely knows his stories keep the two of us connected, and I think sharing them with me gives his life a purpose. That's why he is still taping incidents from his past on the new cassette recorder I bought for him, even though his second stroke continues to affect his speech. Sure, it makes his words a challenge to transcribe, but once I pick up the gist of what he is saying, the content flows. More than anything, I've gleaned a harvest of information that helps me understand my heritage and also why my father, Mike, is the way he is.

Just the other day as I was replacing a cassette full of stories with a new one, I told him how impressed I was with his dedication to our project. Without cracking a smile, he shrugged, and in his post-stroke lingo said, "It fills the time when Annabelle isn't here."

And here I'd expected him to say something profound.

Chapter 4

MIKE O'MALLEY

I haven't been to Highland Manor to see my father, John O'Malley, for two weeks. Since he moved to the nursing home after mother died, I think that's been the longest I've gone without visiting him. I could feel guilty about it, but not seeing him doesn't rank very high on my guilt list because I help him out financially so he can stay in the place. Anyway, with that Negro woman he likes so much encouraging him to get around on his own and Tim's recorder forcing him to speak better, he's actually thriving. He's definitely getting better with or without my visits.

Now, if I could only feel as good about my wife and son. Sara is beyond anyone's help, and Tim doesn't seem to want to connect with me. Normally I'd be pissed off about that except deep down I know I withdrew emotionally from him long before little Marie died. Maybe I was jealous of him because my parents doted on him from the moment he was born...you know, being their only grandchild and all that. Anyway, they moved so much and my dad worked so hard when I was young maybe they thought they'd make it up to me through him. Hell, I don't know what they thought. Anyway, they were good parents. Just not good enough for me, I guess.

What really bothers me is thinking I helped pass on our family's father-son dysfunction. Sadly, in Tim's current state of mind, pushing Michael away is like losing both kids. There's nothing worse than that. But, since I'm not close to Tim, I can't do a darn thing about it. Except, someday I'm going to latch on to that recorder and tell a few stories that I'd never tell him in person. Until then, I'm of a mind-set that life has given up on my Sara and Tim has given up on life. That's why they're both way ahead of my dad on my daily to-do list. He doesn't need me. He probably never has.

At this moment, I'm standing near the open trunk of my new '72 Nash in the parking lot of the Sandy Hollow Golf Course changing into my street shoes. My golf partner, Nels Johnson, who is a good ten years younger than me, is wiping the sweat from his gray crew cut and face with a filthy towel that is attached to his golf bag. I raise an eyebrow, but otherwise say nothing. During the steamy summer months, it's my practice to bring a second clean towel from home just to keep my face and hands dry. Originally it had been one of Sara's better ideas. Now that she isn't around to remind me, I just grab one from the downstairs bathroom each time I leave to play golf.

Our opponents, Charlie and Vince, have already left for the bar at the Swedish Village, and I'm vacillating between dropping Nels off and visiting Sara at the nursing home or joining the three of them for a drink or two. While I struggle into my brown wing tips, Nels hoists both our golf bags into the trunk, being careful to arrange the clubs so that his are on top and easier to lift out when I drive him home. That's one of the duties a grateful partner performs for the day's medalist. The other is collecting the cash from the losing team. Nels grins as he watches me tuck my shoes next to my bag. Then he says, "That was one great round, Mike."

"Thanks," I say patting my face with the towel before tossing it into the upraised trunk onto the tops of my shoes. I sigh. "If I only could have kept my tee shot out of the water on eleven and not three-putted two greens, I could have broken eighty."

Slamming the trunk lid down, Nels moves around the car to the passenger side. "What do you care what you shot, Mike? We won all the money."

"Yeah, but I'm a purist. How I play means more to me than winning."

He groans. "Golf is a game of mistakes for cripes sake. With your attitude you're setting yourself up to be a loser."

I grin. "Now you're catching on, my slow-witted Swedish friend."

Pulling out of the golf course parking lot, I head west on Sandy Hollow toward Eleventh. Nels is still yakking about the round, and I don't interrupt him. As long as I keep his mouth running, I won't have to focus on any of my problems. That was the true purpose behind playing today's four-hour round with my chatty friend. Where else can I spend a half-day immersed in casual banter, or being upset over a sliced drive or missed putt without wanting to get hopelessly drunk? Other than an occasional dinner with my son's family, golf and drink are about my only respites from groveling at the feet of despair. My life hasn't ever been rich with activities like woodworking, playing the piano or other artistic pursuits that shelter some men from their problems. I read the newspaper and *Life Magazine* and listen to the radio in the car, but none of these activities keeps my demons at bay for long. When I awaken each morning, they're always back, and sometimes, I have to fight them hung over. At least with golf I can avoid the hangover. I've learned that much during my sixty-six years.

Even now as my mind wanders from Nels' soliloquy, my problems return to plague me. How am I going to get more orders from customers when the machine tool business is so slow? While I've weathered these downturns before, at my age there's an urgency to fill my coffers. Winter is coming, and I need enough buried nuts to keep my dad in one home, my wife in another and avoid being a burden on Tim, or the State, or whoever takes pity on financial failures. I've been through the Great Depression once. I have no desire to recreate my own personal one.

Nels is still talking, and I'm still saying "uh-huh" in the proper places to let him think I'm listening even though my brain is actually in free-fall. Although it would be rude, I even thought about turning on my White Sox to see how they were faring. Sometimes that diverts my thoughts. Yet, based on the way they've been playing lately, another loss would only add to my funk.

Nels is still back at the course. "Damn, Mike," he's saying. "We really cleaned up today. I won nine bucks, even after losing two side games to those guys. You must have won eleven."

I laughed. "Yeah, a king's ransom. With a fortune like that I can buy you and the other guys a bunch of drinks, a dinner for myself and still have some left over for my piggy bank. We're going to the Swedish Village, aren't we?"

"You worked hard for that dough. I'll buy the drinks so you can put all your winnings into your precious piggy."

"Never thought I'd hear a tightwad Swede say that."

"Cut the Swede crap. If it wasn't for the Swedes in this town, nobody but the old wealth and a few Italians would have any money. All you Irish would be living in shacks and panhandling for drinks. I can see it now. You're standing on the corner of Seventh Street and Third Avenue with your hat in your hand. 'Can you spare a dime so a hard-working Irishman who just shot eighty-two at Sandy Hollow can quench his thirst?'"

I didn't bother to tell him the only thing Irish about me was my name. Actually, I'm Scotch. Still, I really did enjoy having my golf buddy around for comic relief, even if he was just another guy from work, a fellow salesman who called on the same kind of factory accounts as I'd been doing for forty years. However, other than discussing golf and attending the Saturday morning meetings at work where we whispered derisive comments behind the Sales Manager's back, we seldom shared much else of importance. I knew Nels had three kids. The youngest, a boy, was at the University of Illinois. I wasn't sure of his name, but I remembered where he was in school because Nels was always complaining about the cost. "Over fifteen-hundred a year," Nels moaned. "And for what? The kid wants to teach history. At least, he could become an engineer or something where he could make a decent living." As scant as it was, that personal information was more than I ever shared with Nels.

We traveled down Eleventh Street, turned left on Fifth Avenue and in silence headed toward Seventh Street and the Swedish Village. While I admittedly didn't know a whole lot about Nels, I was pleased that he was equally blank about my life. That was by design. I prefer keeping my problems under lock and key. Nels didn't need to know I tried like hell to keep the house up the way Sara would want it, or that my efforts didn't ease my guilt for not visiting her daily. And, even though Tim was doing fine at work and better at home, I worried all the time about his relationship with his son, Michael. Added to that, I get horribly frustrated every time I try to communicate with my aging father who aches for my company at the nursing home. Worst of all, stopping at the Olympic Tavern each night after work for a couple of martinis or shots and beers, depending on my mood, doesn't do anything but dull my senses and add to my guilt.

Ever since I was a kid, I've developed a tactic to steer conversations away from sensitive personal issues with a quip or a joke. Like when my folks came to live with us a few years ago and friends would ask how we were all getting along, I'd say, "Two's company. Four's a crowd," and I'd laugh and let them think it was all working out well when in reality it was so stifling, I could hardly stand it. If I stopped for a beer and a chaser, my mother would smell it on me and say something to my father, who in turn felt like he had to warn me, "If you stop for a drink, please don't be obvious and let your mother know, because she's sure you'll be damned to hell for it, son."

As for the quips and jokes, one time Sara chided me, "You're the only one who thinks you're clever, you know."

"Some people think I am."

"I guess I don't know those people," she said, shaking her head. Then she grinned and kissed me on the cheek. "I do think you're cute most of the time. Anyway, I know you try to say distracting things just to cover up how you really feel."

"Am I good or what!" I said grinning.

"I think you're a WHAT, but I love you anyway." Sara followed up her comments with another kiss.

"That's two for me," I responded before she socked me on the arm and ran into the kitchen laughing.

Now that I can't share precious moments with Sara anymore, I enjoy doing things with acquaintances like Nels. A little golf, a few drinks and no serious conversations that uncover feelings I'd prefer to keep hidden.

I turn left onto Seventh Street and find a parking spot at the curb across from the restaurant/bar. After feeding the meter with change I keep in a small purse in the glove compartment, we cross in the middle of the block and enter the restaurant. With Nels following, I head toward the far end of the large elliptical shaped bar that stands in the center of the room. Booths line the walls and a few four-top wooden tables fill the remaining space. For some reason even though they'd left earlier, the other two guys from the foursome haven't arrived. Before taking a seat next to Nels at the bar, I glance at my watch. Four-forty-five. Enough time for a couple of beers and a meal. Then, I'll go see Sara.

"Any guy that carries his partner by shooting in the low eighties with all your problems deserves a beer. What'll you have, champ?"

"I don't have any problems."

He stares at me and gives a little laugh. "Everybody has problems, you fool," he says. "Anyway, the drink's on me, Mike. Now, what will it be?"

"Schlitz with a shot of Old Crow."

Nels flags the bartender.

"The second is on me," I say.

"Okay, and the third one is on me."

"Then I'll buy dinner, Nels."

"No can do. Lorraine will have the pot on. If I don't make it home, my name is mud." Suddenly, he stands up and waves. "Finally! Here's Charlie and Vince. They must have come by way of Chemung."

I start to pull out a couple of bucks from my wallet to buy a round for our opponents, but Nels grabs my arm. "We have a deal, partner. You got a short memory, or what? This round's on me."

When I reach the bottom of my glass, Charlie and Vince reciprocate, and when I down that one, Nels buys another round. By the time I finish, all three of them are on their feet. "Don't you want a ride home, Nels?" I ask. I am perceptive enough to realize my partner was a lot more excited about riding with me to the tavern than letting me drive him home.

"No problem, Mike. Vince goes right by my place. Just bring my clubs to work in the morning, and I'll transfer them to my trunk at lunch time." Then as an afterthought, he says, "You won't get in an accident, will ya?"

I shake my head and raise my glass to them as they depart.

Instantly feeling very alone, I order another beer and carry it with me to a booth. By then the hands on the wall clock are straight up and down. After a quick dinner, I still have time to see Sara before visiting hours are over. Opening the menu, I glance at the white card clipped to the inside of the cover. Tonight's special is roast beef with mashed potatoes, gravy and green beans. I order it along with another beer and chaser.

When I finally leave the Swedish Village, it's way past visiting hours and too late to visit Sara, so I carefully guide the Nash home. Actually, by then I am too mellow to feel bad about it. She never knows whether I'm there or not anyway.

The next day after making my last call on the purchasing agent at Ingersoll, instead of stopping at the nearby Olympic Tavern, my guilt from the previous night drives me to visit my wife first and stop for a drink later. When I arrive at the small single-story complex, I pass through the lobby where heartier but much older residents than my wife are chatting and watching TV. From there I head down the hall, bracing myself for what I'll see when I enter her room. Invariably, seeing Sara strapped into a wheelchair with her vacant eyes open and her head tilted to the side almost resting on her shoulder brings tears. Today is no exception. After wiping them away with a knuckle, I greet her, "Hi Honey, it's Mike."

Nothing.

The disease had begun simply enough with little memory lapses like forgetting names and directions to familiar locations like the grocery store or gas station. As she regressed, she'd sometimes stare at a sink full of soapy dishes with a perplexed look on her face unable to remember what to do next. Or, she'd put on a skirt and her hose and high heels and then come sauntering down the stairs from her bedroom wearing only her bra and a big smile from the waist up. Each of these incidents were just happenings that we'd laugh about. Never once did I show her the concern I was feeling, preferring to pretend they were nothing. However, below the surface her lapses scared the shit out of me.

Then she got worse. When she started driving on the wrong side of the street either speeding or driving five miles per hour, I took away her car. Then there were the times she didn't know her name. One day she'd be Carole, the next Bernice. She was seldom Sara. Other days she wouldn't know my name, and when I'd remind her it was Mike, she'd get angry and say in a tone unfamiliar to me, "I know who you are." That anger was what really broke me up. My princess had always been spunky, but she usually had a smile on her face. She never yelled at me.

Finally, she began wandering off and getting lost whenever I wasn't around to keep tabs on her, and I knew something had to be done. At first, I tried to keep her at home with a care-giver, but it was awkward having my parents and the woman around, and expensive, too. As the disease progressed, Sara became so totally unmanageable, the woman quit. That forced me to place her in the dementia unit.

Today's lack of response was now the norm. She hadn't responded to anything I'd said for the last six months or so. If she knew I existed at all, our history together was hidden under so many layers of dying cells, she'd never have the ability to remember it. Even though I'd given up trying to rekindle the intimacy between us that sustained me for over forty years, I always carried a faint hope that sometime when I was near she'd be her old self again. Early on she had lots of lucid moments. At times, she'd smile at me. Once in awhile she'd curse her fate. But, as time went by, these windows into her mind were shuttered, and she'd become the lifeless vegetative figure I now saw before me.

Lately, I began to wish she'd die so I could wallow in my good memories. I knew eventually God would take her like He took every other creature. There were a few weak moments when, if I had it in me, I'd have helped Him. But I never did. I endured each vigil sitting on the edge of her bed feeling helpless and hopeless and giving my tears full reign. Then, I'd eventually leave like I was about to do tonight, have a few drinks to improve my outlook so that if I ran into someone who asked about her, I could fake a smile and say she was doing as well as could be expected.

Some days, unlike today, I'd let anger well up inside me to the point I'd rail at a fiendish God who'd let this sweet soul disintegrate into such a mindless zombie. What had she ever done to deserve such a tragic ending? Pick's disease, they called it. A Jewish disease that began to manifest itself before she turned sixty. A premature senility that blanked her mind and features and eventually ripped her from me.

I wondered at times if God was upset because she hadn't practiced her Jewish faith. Nonsense. Neither had her parents. Her mother hadn't since she was a child. Her father, never. Certainly, He didn't care that she wasn't faithful to her ancestors' beliefs, especially since she'd been true to Him as a Christian follower. Hell, when she was well, I was never as devout as she was. So, why this ending? And, why do I have to sit here and watch her fade away?

21

I slip from the bed and push her wheelchair to the window. Then, I pull a small chair next to her and gaze out over the asphalt parking lot to the cars and trucks speeding by on Riverside. Maybe I should have bitten the bullet and placed her in one of those more expensive homes like the one my father dwells in. There's a vast expanse of green grass there, and trees and birds my father can't even see. Sara loved birds, but there aren't any to watch except for possibly a few pigeons. Maybe she'd emerge from her fog if there were robins and cardinals and finches flitting around her window.

With tears welling up in my eyes, I reach over and pick up her hand. "I'm so sorry, Honey."

That's when I feel her gentle squeeze.

Chapter 5

JOHN O'MALLEY

Annabelle was in earlier today. Besides making my bed and tidying up, she said I should be walking a bit more to keep up my strength. I don't know if the doctor suggested it, or she decided it on her own, but I like the idea. She holds onto my arm and spends a lot more time with me than usual. So, even if I end up in a heap on the floor, I'm all for trying.

Sometimes after she leaves, I feel so much joy I laugh out loud. That feels good. Old men should laugh when they can. If we don't, our throats dry up and our lungs fill with phlegm. The same with crying. Since I can't see much, it's good to know those useless holes in my skull are good for something.

I cried a lot after Florence died. What a woman. She traipsed all around the country with me as I went from one job to the next. First Maine, where we were married, then Boston, Baltimore, New York City and back to Baltimore. A year here, a couple of years there, moving from one apartment to another making a home for Mike, our son, and me. Then East St. Louis, Calumet City, Chicago, Cleveland and Milwaukee, before I hung up my tool-belt in Michigan. Much later, after keeping up our home, large yard and vegetable garden got to be too much, Mike invited us to live with him in Rockford. He wanted to keep an eye on us, he said. Actually I think Mike wanted us to keep an eye on his wife, Sara, who was all deranged long before she was eligible for Social Security.

Then Flo had a heart attack and died. Considering she had asthma and had been diagnosed with leukemia, I was glad she didn't have to suffer anymore. Although I uttered those words to make Mike and Tim think her death was a blessing, my comments rang false in my ears. Even worse, I doubt my words soothed either of them a whit. I sure as hell know my words didn't describe the devastation I felt in my soul.

My first thought was to bury her back near her parents in Kittery Point, but after my second stroke, how could a blind-mute make the arrangements to have her buried in Maine. So, I made the decision to place her in a local Rockford cemetery with an empty space next to her for me. Since we've lived about everywhere, I felt Rockford was as good a place as any for us to be planted. What a future. Side by side for all eternity–Flo and me. Just as it's always been.

I especially liked the idea when I was told our plot was near the site where my grandson Tim's little daughter, Marie, was buried. Poor sweet tyke. I held her in my arms a few times when we used to visit from Michigan, and she'd giggle and place her tiny arms around my neck, and best of all, she never grabbed my glasses like most little children did. Those were good times. Little Marie in my arms, Flo standing over me throwing out warnings not to crush the child, and Tim laughing at an old man who is lovin' every minute of it.

Yep, I feel good about those memories until I stop to think that here I am hanging on in my nineties while Tim's a miserable mess at times because my great-granddaughter never made it past five and a half. Where's the justice in that? If this were the turn of the century when lots of kids died, I'd understand it better, but it isn't. It's the nineteen seventies. They've got antibiotics, and other things, but evidently her case was so rampant that if the doctor could have saved her she might have been blind and like Sara. In the end, the doctor couldn't save my great-granddaughter anyway, and it sent Tim and his wife into a downward spiral that has profoundly affected their marriage and his relationship with his son, my only great-grandson, Michael.

However, I do think Tim's learning to cope a little bit. He really seems to like writing up my stories, and he's good at writing so I think that makes him happy. Whether I'm right I'm not sure, but I do know telling them is helping me.

Unlike this old sandhog, I'm not sure Tim can deal with big setbacks. Starting with my childhood in Augusta, Maine, whenever bad things have happened in my life, I just assumed they were meant to be and moved on. That's how I landed in Kittery Point in 1897. Or, like now, maybe a stroke might bring some men down, or being unable to see much might cause another to give up. But, not me. With my goggles on, I can see enough light and shadows to know I'm not stuffed into a casket, and learning to talk again is a challenge I willingly embrace. Why? It's simple. Since I don't know what my destiny is meant to be, I sure as hell don't want to miss anything I'm supposed to experience. What if Annabelle plants a kiss on my forehead again, or Tim comes around for *story time,* or I get a chance to chew Mike's butt for drinking too much? I wouldn't want to miss any of that. Or, maybe the doctors will come up with something that will fix my eyes so I can play cribbage again and find a way to keep me from having another stroke. Hell, in that case, I just might want to live forever.

With the exception of those two guys who couldn't help Marie up in Michigan, I've personally always had good luck with doctors. Back in Maine, they were always fixing me up, usually because I had been doing some darn fool thing. For example, there was the time in the middle of December, 1902, when I was almost twenty. I was sitting bare-headed and bare-handed in a tree stand in the middle of Carson's Woods waiting for a deer to come by. Unlike the stupid kids today that wear only a tee shirt while they stand in a snow drift waiting on the corner for their yellow school bus, I knew better. Even though my mother had died the day I was born, all through my childhood I received warnings from her through my dad just like the other kids who actually had living mothers. "Dress warmly, son," was one of the warnings I heard often. However, do you think I'd hear her voice in the wilderness that day? Hell, no! Nothing was going to drive me back to the cabin to get a hat and gloves. Why? It was simple. I was nineteen, I was omnipotent, and I was sure a whole herd of deer was about to show up in front of my perch. Why would I let a little cold weather keep me from shooting a big buck? As fate would have it, the deer never showed. All I had to show for my foolishness was a case of frostbite that turned my fingers and the tops of my ears blue and blistered the skin on my face; a freezer-burn that could have killed me if it got infected, or I caught a cold that turned into pneumonia.

Good old Doc Warner knew what to do, though. After my future father-in-law, Mr. Ferland, fetched him in the one-horse rig and brought him to his hunting cabin, he soaked my hands in cool water and held cool then hot compresses against my face and ears gradually returning the skin to a normal temperature. It seemed like he was there for hours but it probably was half that. Then he gave me aspirin to take now and later and told me just not to be so stupid again. Looking back, I owe him far more than the dollar and the side of venison Mr. Ferland promised him for keeping me alive. Back then a lot of guys died. I know, because I buried a bunch of buddies.

In Baltimore it was old Doctor James who sewed up and bandaged all my work injuries. One time he even removed a bass plug that had been hanging from my nose for three hours while Otis Lundy and I raced my Model T back from a pond on an acquaintance's farm in Virginia where we'd been fishing. Removing the plug was especially painful because the barb was stuck in the inside of my nostril. To free it, Doctor James had to pull the pointed hook all the way through the skin until the barb was on the outside of my nose. Then he cut off the barb with a small tin snip and backed what was left of the wire out through the entry hole until the plug was free. After that, he covered his work with iodine. I remember because it stung like hell.

I don't see my great-grandson, Michael, much because he's away at college. That's understandable, but I'm a little surprised his mother, Claire, seldom shows up. That's sad, too, because I like her a lot, and she likes me. Still, I guess I understand. When a marriage is in crisis, the debris hits everyone. Hopefully, that will change. My real hope is Michael stays close to both his parents, and maybe sometime when he's home from college he'll pop in on me. Even though I can't see well enough to play cribbage with him anymore or speak well enough to make myself understood just yet, I still should be able to let him know how much I care about him. That's important, because even though I'm difficult company, I want him to think well of me. Then again, if he doesn't come by, I'll still have my memories of Michael when he was younger and his parents were happy and his baby sister was alive. Most of the time, that's enough for this old sandhog.

Chapter 6

John O'Malley

Annabelle must have the day off because the white one has been in several times already. She made the bed and pushed me down to breakfast herself instead of telling the orderlies to do it. They're both good guys except they speak Spanish, I think, and I can't understand a word they say. Kind of makes us even, I guess, because they can't understand me either. Hardly anyone can, except Tim and Annabelle.

After breakfast, when *Snow White* was bringing me back to the room, she was chattering away like a jay. Since she was so unusually friendly, I couldn't help but think she must have got some last night. Back in the room she wheeled me directly into the "john" and helped me onto the pot for my morning dump. I've noticed with both Annabelle and this one that my dump seems to be an important part of their day. While I'm not against a good one, it doesn't hold the same fascination for me as it does for them. The same with my peeing. I guess there's something in their nursing creed that stresses the importance of elimination, but I feel they're a bit obsessed with it.

When *WE'RE* done, she helps me shower, brush my teeth and change into some clean clothes. Just by the way she tosses me around like a feather, she's got to be half-gorilla or strong as an ox. She's sure not someone I want for an enemy. Since I'm aware of her moods, I decide it might be wise to know her name so I can butter her up a little bit. That way if she's having a bitchy day, maybe

29

she won't hurt me, and if she's in a good mood, we can have some fun together to pass the time. The problem is how to proceed when I'm saddled with poor eyesight and mostly unintelligible speech.

My opening comes when she lifts me up and stands about two feet away facing me. I catch a glimpse of what I presume is a name tag and point to it. "Wasynam," I ask. However, instead of touching the plastic tag, my finger plunges into a soft pillow of flesh. It feels like tit to me.

She takes a startled step back and leaves me teetering. Knowing my history with her, I fully expect her to let me topple onto the floor and leave me there before storming out of the room. But no, she grabs hold of me with both hands and steadies me. Then, she laughs and helps me into my wheelchair. Her laugh is no guffaw, mind you, just a tight embarrassed giggle, but it continues for quite awhile until she says, "Oh, Mr. O'Malley, I wish I knew what you'd said."

Since she'd left me an opening to redeem myself, I repeat my question very slowly, "Was-y-nam."

I hear her chuckle. "Oh, I see. You want to know my name. Well, it's Alice. Alice Borowski."

I smile and repeat, "Al-ice?"

And she says, "That's right."

Fortunately, I don't have to deal with the Borowski.

For the rest of the morning she was sweet as pie. Then, before she left, she said, "Oh darn, I'm sorry Mr. O'Malley. I forgot to tell you, your son called, and he's going to have dinner with you here tonight. Isn't that great?"

I nodded, and then after she left I thought about how nice Alice had been all morning, and I knew for sure she'd gotten some last night.

Too bad, Mike never showed. It's been quite awhile since we shared a meal. I guess he must have gotten tied up with a customer, or stopped at the tavern or something. If I could have eaten with him instead of the old farts, it would have been a near perfect day even without seeing Annabelle.

Chapter 7

THE DIARY OF A SANDHOG

While I tend to tell folks I'm from Kittery Point, I actually was born and lived on a farm near Augusta. That's in Maine, too. I never knew my mother because she died giving birth to me. I guess that's why my older brother, Jacob, resented me. I certainly never did anything else to justify his sour feelings other than being born. The worst part was whenever there was friction between us, which was often, our father always sided with him. As hard as I tried, I never could win over our pop so I could stand on equal footing with Jacob.

In 1898 when I was sixteen, I finally realized my father only had room in his heart for one son. So, I quit school and cleaned out my savings account. Then I slipped up to the attic and permanently borrowed my father's brown leather bag. After filling it with a couple of shirts, a pair of pants, some clean underwear and a bar of soap, I left home in the middle of the night. For no reason other than I needed to make some money to get to Boston or some other big city where I intended to find work, I headed south along the coast and stopped in Kittery Point. As it turned out, I found far more there than a temporary job.

It all began on the day I arrived in town when I ran into a tall, graying and courtly man at the coffee shop. His name was George Ferland. I began chatting with him over a donut and coffee and took an immediate liking to him. For some reason, he also took an interest in me. From our conversation, he must have guessed at my willingness to do grunt work for the lowest hourly wage known to man. However, I think it was something more than that. I think he simply liked me and wanted to help me out.

Within weeks, I was learning at the feet of a world-class carpenter, and he found out I had a strong back and never tired. After two months, I became his apprentice, and he began teaching me the tricks of his trade. Over time, with the successful completion of each job, we grew more dependent on each other. We also grew closer. Rather than boss and laborer, he treated me more like the son he never had. At the same time, he became the father figure I always wanted, and Kittery Point became my hometown and point of reference for the rest of my life. As a consequence, I never returned to Augusta or planned to lay eyes on my father or my brother, Jacob, again. I also never sent them so much as a penny postcard to let them know my whereabouts, nor, to my knowledge, did either of them ever try to contact me.

Instead of moving on, I stayed in Kittery Point to learn everything I could from Mr. Ferland. That first summer he taught me the rudiments of his trade. The next year I became a carpenter. Over time I hoped to become as fine a craftsman as my teacher. Evidently I was capable in his eyes, because as I became more skilled, he raised my wages.

That fall as the winds off the Atlantic blew through the walls of the cheap, poorly heated boarding house where I had settled when I first came to Kittery Point, Mr. Ferland gave me an unexpected gift. He and Mrs. Ferland invited me to move into a comfortable room in the attic of their large white clapboard house on the bay. They also insisted I take my meals with them. The remarkable aspect of the arrangement was they offered me the new digs at no cost to me just like I was family. I was thrilled! Live for free, and save every penny I earned to finance my future–whatever and wherever that might be.

However, there was one downside to my new living arrangement. Their daughter, Florence, was fourteen, an only child and a real pest. She did her best to torment me whenever she could, and I tolerated her only because she came with the gift.

After I'd been living with the Ferlands for almost two years, they began dropping hints that I should get back into high school and pick up where I'd left off in Augusta. At first their suggestions fell on deaf ears. I never liked school much. Plus, with the good deal I'd fallen into, I couldn't see any purpose in it. How learned did a guy have to be to work with his hands and back? In my mind, I didn't need to know algebra, or world history or the poetry of some long dead English writer. Still, as time went by, Mr. and Mrs. Ferland became more and more insistent, and I didn't understand why.

Sometime over the next year or so I figured it out. They were good observers. They'd seen my feelings toward their daughter change from irritation to interest, and hers from little sister tormentor to teenage temptress. They saw the possibility that our relationship might stay the course and blossom, and if that were to happen, they certainly didn't want a son-in-law who was dumb as a stump and less educated than their only daughter no matter how hard a worker he might be. Stubborn as I was, I fought them off for as long as I could, but in the end I went back to high school.

As a reward, my mentor cut my hours so I could attend classes and do my homework. By the time I graduated, he had raised my hourly rate enough so my savings hardly suffered. I'm sure the fact I was a saver boded well in their minds should Flo and I ever get seriously involved. But, of course, nothing like that was ever said in my presence.

Chapter 8

John O'Malley

Tim visited me earlier today and read me some of the Kittery Point stories he took off the recorder. I'll have to admit they brought tears to my eyes. How that boy can get my story just right from my garbled speech is amazing. Plus, he seems as happy doing it as I feel when I eat a delicious Maine lobster. Anyway, I'm glad I'm pleasing him, because everything he writes is just the way I remember it.

Chapter 9

THE DIARY OF A SANDHOG

I'm afraid Mr. Ferland is rapidly aging. I can tell by the way he huffs and puffs and shuffles from spot to spot when he's on the job. His strength, which when I joined him four years ago had been impressive, has now diminished to the point where he can no longer hold up a ridge board with one hand and nail his end of the rafter with the other. More and more, he's leaving all the heavy work for me while he does the trim, builds the cabinets and supervises me. He's also soliciting fewer jobs. Mr. Ferland always says he's been stashing away greenbacks for his old age, so it occurs to me that he might be taking on less work by design. After all, he is fifty-five. I hope I'm not working construction when I'm that old.

This last year in Kittery Point has been a difficult one for me. On the good side, Florence and I have pledged our love for one another. On the other, because her father's business is wilting, and I'm not experienced enough to take it over and make it prosper again, my future in Kittery Point looks bleak. The sad truth is, in 1901 with my limited skills, no matter how industrious I might be, I could never support a wife for long without relying on her dad's charity. Florence has even said as much in one of our quiet evening chats. "If Papa winds down his business, he'll take care of us until you find another good job here in Kittery."

"There are no good jobs in Kittery Point for guys like me," I told her. "If he closes his business, we'll have to move to Boston or somewhere else to find work."

"But, I don't want to leave home," she whimpered.

I hate it when girls whimper. It's not fighting fair. So, I fixed her by saying, "Then I guess you want me for a brother, not a husband." While my words stunned her, the kiss I planted on her lips ended the discussion and brought back her smile. I followed with, "No grown man should ever live off another man's generosity. At least, I can't and won't." That left her all mixed up and worried again.

Financial considerations aside, our blissful road to the altar had been strewn with boulders placed there by our own over-zealous desires. For some time, Flo had been sneaking up the steps to my attic room in the dead of night. While her parents were most likely oblivious to our midnight meetings and the chances of their finding us together in that spread out house were minimal, we had been on the brink of taking other risks during our passionate moments. Of course, we'd never go beyond our self-imposed limit, because we were afraid of an unwanted result.

In that community of God-fearing Puritans, an out-of-wedlock pregnancy would disgrace the Ferlands, tarnish Flo's previously pristine reputation and hasten a private church ceremony where the pastor would quickly make the marriage legal. Following the service, we'd be given a few bucks to tide us over and hustled out of town on the next train south. Then I'd have to find a job that paid enough to support a family of three. What was worse would be my betrayal of the family that took me in and treated me like a son. No matter how much passion I felt for Flo, I could never do anything that would hurt them.

Of course, none of our fears put an end to our midnight meetings. They only placed limits on them.

In early March, Flo and I decided I should leave Kittery Point alone to seek my fortune in Boston where I could likely find a good-paying job. Then, once I'd pocketed a few paychecks, I'd return for a traditional church wedding where her father would give her away, and she could wear the white wedding dress she'd always dreamed of followed by a one night honeymoon in a hotel on the way to our new home.

After the pact was sealed with a kiss, Flo left my bedroom with a final plea, "You will come and get me as soon as you can, won't you, John? You won't forget our promise? I am almost eighteen."

I answered, "Of course I will be back for you," because I understood a woman's fear of becoming an old maid. Besides, I was deeply in love with Flo and every day away from her would be less than a perfect one.

The next day when I casually laid out my plans for leaving Kittery Point, Mr. Ferland readily admitted out loud what Flo and I already suspected. "I've been winding down my business, John. I thought about letting you take it over, but I felt you were too inexperienced. Some day when you've learned the financial aspects of carpentry, you can come back, and if I'm still around, I'll help you start your own business. You're a good man, John." Then, while the women prepared dinner, he took me aside and attempted a brief tutorial on the art of finding and holding a job in the construction industry in Boston.

Two mornings later, I left Kittery Point driving the horse and buggy to the train station in Portsmouth with Florence by my side. I was excited. With her father's wisdom packed away, I knew that Boston offered me the opportunities and independence I craved. For the moment, at least, I was more excited about the future in the big city than sad about leaving this idyllic coastal town. How could I feel sad? I knew in my heart I'd always be returning to Kittery Point because I would always be welcome there. Unlike my escape from Augusta four years before, I wasn't running away from a place and people I couldn't abide. I was riding into a new life with blessings and a satchel full of wonderful memories. Plus, before long, I'd be back for Flo, we'd be married and my life would be complete. Following our parting kisses at the railway station, I couldn't wait to prove to myself the decision I had made was the correct one.

Chapter 10

The Diary of a Sandhog

Once the train departed from the Portsmouth station for Boston, I was immersed in comfort. A large measure of that comfort came from knowing what was buried deep within my right-hand pants pocket. Glancing around at the half-empty car of disinterested passengers, I went fishing for the bank savings account book I'd stashed there. I peeked at the monumental total, $134.14. This lifetime of savings would provide the safety net should a month go by without my finding work. For good measure, I took out my wallet crammed full of greenbacks as a result of my final two week's wages and a generous parting gift from Mr. Ferland. There I found another $104 plus the change jingling in my pocket. This accounting was the third of the day. The first had been when I'd awakened, and the second when I was whiling away my time in the bathroom. While it gave me comfort to know I had this fortune tucked away, I was a bit taken back by the cost of the six dollar train ticket.

On the fabric seat next to me, a cardboard box added to my comfort. So I wouldn't starve, Mrs. Ferland had packed it with cheeses and breads, cakes and cookies and enough home preserved vegetables to last me a week or more. My father's worn leather grip held my meager wardrobe, and it lay on the floor under my seat. The bag was the last remnant of my earlier life in Augusta. I found it intriguing that without it I might not have been able to make a quick escape. Studying it, I wondered if later he considered my theft a small price to pay to end our stormy relationship. Or, was it possible he considered it a cheap going away present. Either way, I'm sure he has no regrets over my leaving. Nor do I.

When the colored porter came by hawking food and drinks, I reached into my pants pocket and pulled out a nickel. In return, I received a wide smile, a "Thank you, sir" and a newly uncapped bottle of Coca-Cola. After I carefully placed the bottle against the back of the empty seat next to me, I dug into the box of food. Using my pocket knife, I soon made a makeshift sandwich of brick cheese and homemade bread. Then, before taking a sip or eating a bite, I ran my tongue over my lips to savor the remnant of Flo's last kiss. For the remainder of the one-hour trip, I munched the sandwich, drank the cola and watched the Holstein-filled fields glide by my window without giving further thought to what lay ahead.

When I disembarked the train at South Station, the first thing I did was buy a *Globe* with the two pennies I pulled from my pocket. Standing in the center of the lobby with people rushing by me in all directions, I opened it up. I skipped over the front page because I wasn't particularly interested in how President Teddy Roosevelt was running the country at that moment, and I didn't dwell on the sports page because I'd already heard someone say the Boston Beaneaters had won 6-4. Instead, I began searching the want-ads for construction jobs and rooms for rent.

Before I'd left, Mr. Ferland had suggested I concentrate my efforts in places like Brookline and Waltham. "Those are growing areas," he'd said. "That's where the builders will be eager to hire a strong, hard-working young man like you."

With help from several strangers who seemed to pop up out of nowhere to lend assistance, I finally found the streetcar stop for a tram whose end destination was in the heart of the area I planned on canvassing. With the newspaper tucked into my rear pocket, my small suitcase in one hand and the box of food under my other arm, I climbed aboard the car and found an empty wooden seat. Throughout the entire half-hour trip, I read the ads and circled the ones that appeared to offer the best prospects for work and the cheapest places to live. When the streetcar finally clanged for the last time announcing the end of the line, I got off and found myself standing on the sidewalk facing Newton Street in Brookline.

I was in awe. In all of my twenty years I'd never seen anything in Augusta or Kittery or even Portsmouth that rivaled the scene that lay before me. Towering new three and four-story buildings sprouted from the edges of the sidewalk in bunches. In the open spaces between, large old single-family homes loomed. These homes were all that was left to remind visitors of what the street had looked like in the last half of the nineteenth century.

While I was gawking, a carriage with a team of horses straining at their reins flew past me and careened around the corner. A block or so later, I came across an old mare laboring at a snail's pace pulling a wagon full of junk. The contrast fascinated me. However, neither captured my imagination like seeing a horseless carriage putt-putting up the street moments later. I couldn't help but chuckle at the idea of a buggy propelling itself. I'd seen pictures of this new invention, but until I actually saw that quaint vehicle driving down Newton Street, I never really believed such a thing existed. The funniest part of the whole drama came when the driver of the autocar squeezed his high-pitched air horn to warn the driver of the slow-moving wagon he was passing him by. Now that was really something.

My goal for the afternoon was to check out a couple of the rooming houses I'd found in the newspaper. However, after I began to realize I might be lost, I stopped a pedestrian and asked him where 2104 Oxford Street might be. The man shook his head thoughtfully and gestured in the general direction of where I was headed. "It's off to the right up ahead, me thinks." Assessing his indecision, I tried to determine whether he really knew the way or not. The answer became clear when he stroked his grizzled chin and added, "To be on the safe side, ye better ask someone else." Since no one else was in my proximity, I picked up my belongings and forged ahead in the direction I'd been traveling all along.

In short order, I saw three burley young men in work-clothes walking toward me in the street singing at the top of their lungs. They were joined arm-in-arm and laughing. Since I felt surely one of them would help me, I took a few steps toward the street to block their path intending to ask for directions. When they didn't part or slow up, I realized their intent might be to run me over or knock me down and quickly moved aside. As it was, one of them laughed and tried to kick the suitcase out of my hand as he passed, but missed. It suddenly occurred to me that these might be the hooligans full of drink Mr. Ferland had warned me about. The realization made me feel fortunate the three of them didn't decide to turn around and beat me up.

Eventually, I found Oxford Street, and I rang the bell at the corner house, 2104. A woman cracked the door and peered out at me. "State your business, young man." Evidently the words came out a little harsher than she intended, because after a pause she said, "May I help you?"

I waved the newspaper in front of me. "I'm here about your room."

"Oh, I'm sorry. I let it this morning."

"I'm sorry, too. Your home looks very nice, and I wanted to live in this area."

She opened the door a bit farther and said, "Where are you from?"

"Maine. Originally Augusta. Most recently, Kittery Point. I'm looking for work in the construction field. I'm an apprentice carpenter, and I'm hoping to find a good job so my wife-to-be can join me." I smiled at her. "I've only been gone since this morning, and I already miss my Florence."

She laughed. "What a coincidence! My name is Florence, too. Florence Baker. You seem like a nice young man, Mr...?"

"John O'Malley."

"Mr. O'Malley. Just out of curiosity, what are you planning on paying for a room?"

Since I hadn't really given much thought to my housing budget, I thought a second and threw out a number. "Four dollars a week?"

Evidently my answer pleased her because she said, "Won't you come in and chat for a few moments, John O'Malley?"

"I'd certainly enjoy the opportunity to get better acquainted, Mrs. Baker, but considering I have no place to sleep tonight or the next, I'd better be going."

"I was thinking about that myself, Mr. O'Malley. That's why I'm inviting you in. I may have a solution to your problem." She opened the door all the way and motioned me inside. "Do you like tea, John O'Malley?" When I nodded, she took my grip and my box of food and placed them on the floor of the foyer. Then she pointed toward a chair in the parlor and said, "I'll put the pot on and join you shortly."

Since I had few other options at the moment, I chose to be compliant. Afterwards, I was glad I decided to have that cup of tea because in the conversation that accompanied it, I learned about "a neighbor who has a lovely room that's just longing for a gentleman guest like you." To further my cause with the neighbor who had always been reluctant to rent out her spare room, my new friend, Mrs. Florence Baker, entreated me to pick up my belongings. Then, she took me by the arm and walked me over to 2116 Oxford Street and introduced me to Elizabeth Borden.

"Betty, I've just let your back bedroom to Mr. John O'Malley here. He's your new tenant."

The startled woman accepted my hand and asked me in at which point Mrs. Baker turned on her heel and headed home. "You can thank me later, Betty," she said as she departed and left Mrs. Borden and I gawking at each other in the hallway of her large two-story Victorian home. Then, just like Mrs. Baker, she invited me to have tea.

That same evening after asking me a few questions and touching on a few house rules, she escorted me up a wide staircase to a large, immaculate bedroom toward the back of her home. The first thing I noticed was the ornate print wall covering and dark molding where the ceiling met the walls. I also observed the white crocheted bedspread covering the blue blanket that adorned the double bed. The highlight of the tour for me, however, was the bathroom off the hall that she and I would be sharing. With all the cola and tea I'd been pouring into my system, I could barely wait for Mrs. Borden to retreat to her parlor so I could use it in privacy.

The cost. Four dollars per week for the room. Seven dollars including breakfast and dinner. Even if I couldn't immediately find a job, I could stay a month or more with just the money in my wallet.

Unlike Florence Baker, who was just knocking on the door of middle-age, the white-haired Mrs. Borden was quite elderly. Judging from her stooped posture and the stories she told me about her experiences during the Civil War, I assumed she might conceivably be in her sixties. Still, she wasn't as doddering as some other very old people I'd met. In fact, I found out later when she'd have a wee nip before dinner, she could be quite lively.

During that first month, she soon became the mother I never had. Possibly because she'd never had a tenant before, she treated me like family, cooking the foods I liked to eat and, even though it wasn't part of the contract, making my bed. In addition, she and also Mrs. Baker, kept an eye and an ear out for any job opportunities and passed them on to me. In return, I'd sit in the parlor with my hostess and share my life history and future plans with her. I'd also help with the dishes and keep her little patch of grass mowed. And, of course, I wrote about all my experiences in my nightly letter to Flo.

One late afternoon, after I'd been pounding the pavement introducing myself to the owners of several small construction firms with no success, the doorbell rang. Since Mrs. Borden was in the kitchen cooking chowder, I moved from my chair in the parlor and answered it. Opening the door, I towered over a young uniformed telegraph delivery boy. In a squeaky voice he said, "Telegram for John O'Malley."

"I'm John O'Malley."

"Sign here, please," he said, placing a small book and a pencil in my hand. When I finished, he rummaged around in a leather bag that hung from his shoulder, took out an envelope and handed it to me. Taking it, I fished two pennies from my pocket and placed them in his hand along with the book and pencil. "God bless you, sir," he hollered over his shoulder as he trotted toward his bicycle lying on its side on the walk. I watched as he picked it up and rode off.

Standing in the doorway fingering the envelope, my gut churned. I'd never received a telegram before and my anxieties waged a war against opening it. In my mind it could only be bad news. Weighing the possibility that some employer had accepted my application and I'd soon have a job, against some frightful message from Flo or Mr. Ferland, I assumed the worst. Moreover, since no one else I'd ever left behind cared enough about me to send such an expensive message, I mentally narrowed my choices between the best and worst options. Then, before returning to the parlor, I gritted my teeth, tore open the envelope and took out the message.

I read it once in disbelief. Then, I read it a second time and burst out laughing. It was from Flo.

John - stop - You are in mortal danger - stop - Lizzie Borden killed her father and stepmother with an ax - stop - Move at once - stop - Florence.

Later that night I sat down and wrote Flo. Besides pouring out my heart to her as I usually did, I thanked her for looking out for my well-being. I then wrote this addendum.

In 1894 when Lizzie Borden supposedly committed her act of violence, [she was acquitted by the way] she was around thirty-years-old. That would now make her about forty. My sweet Elizabeth

Borden is probably in excess of sixty and would have trouble swinging an ax. While Lizzie Borden lived in Fall River, Massachusetts, about fifty miles south of here, Elizabeth Borden lives at 2116 Oxford Street in Brookline, Massachusetts. Finally, many people call my landlord Betty, but I've never heard anyone call her Lizzie. Do not fear, I am not in mortal danger from Mrs. Borden.

    All my love,
    John

Chapter 11

THE DIARY OF A SANDHOG

I surrendered my life to Boomer McHale one evening in mid-April of 1902 when he stopped by unannounced to visit his mother's sister, sweet old Mrs. Borden. He was a hod-carrier by trade in the old country, and a roustabout turned sandhog by financial necessity in his adopted land. Tall for an Irishman, he was probably about thirty or so, barrel-chested with biceps as large as the lower branches of a five-hundred-year-old oak. And, he was loud. With an indecipherable brogue, even his whisper would fill the Boston Cathedral with enough racket to disrupt a Sunday service.

When Thomas, the name used by his aunt, arrived, he embraced her slight frame so tightly I would have thought her lungs would collapse from the pressure. But, after a couple of gasps she quickly recovered, and I stopped worrying about her out of concern for what he had in store for me. I soon found out when he took a step back, studied me for a moment and uttered something in an amused brogue that sounded like, "Well, what is this thing here?"

"This is John O'Malley, Thomas, the boy I told your mother about."

"Aye. I'm pleased to meet him, then." Anticipating the worst, I hesitantly stuck out my hand. While he was crushing it, I'd swear I heard every bone crack. However, by the time Mrs. Borden had

49

guided us into the parlor, the initial pain had been reduced to a soothing numbness.

I found a spot on the sofa next to Mrs. Borden and remained quiet as the big man talked his way into a dainty, blue-velvet side chair across from us. Mrs. Borden eyed his bulk and suggested, "It might be better for my antique chair, Thomas, if we exchanged seats." However, neither stopped talking long enough to make the switch. I was glad. Watching and listening to them as they brought each other up to date on various family members, I learned a lot about each of their histories. I also discovered a softer version of the man emerging from his crude veneer.

Interrupting them from time to time, I learned that Mrs. Borden and Thomas' mother, Kathleen, along with their parents had emigrated to Boston in the eighteen-fifties from County Clare following the Irish potato famine. Over the next fifty plus years, Elizabeth Borden lived a life that was much different from Kathleen's and the majority of her former countrymen. She not only graduated from high school and attended the University of Massachusetts in Andover, but she became a teacher in the small town of Beverly. In time, she married a well-to-do storekeeper there, gave up teaching and had one son. Sadly, she lost her husband at forty-eight to a heart attack. Since she had neither the interest in nor the ability to run a retail men's clothing store, she sold it to her son, Sean, and moved in with him, his wife, Mary, and their daughter, Eileen, "in this very same house in Brookline."

By contrast, Kathleen, who was four years younger than her sister never broke away from her parents, and, like them, never fully adjusted to living in America. Never a good student, Kathleen left school at barely sixteen. In order to support herself, she found work as a live-in domestic at the home of a well-off Brahmin family in Boston.

While she was chafing under her employer's stringent rules, their parents moved to Springfield, Massachusetts where their father found work at a company that manufactured rifles. During the Civil War, the business boomed and immigrants from all over the world were sought after to work there. However, when the "war between the states" ended, the job picture changed. The young fighting men who'd saved the country from splitting in two needed jobs. To reward these returning heroes and at the same time rid themselves of the vexing problems caused by the troublesome, annoying foreigners who didn't speak the language, many companies, including the rifle plant in Springfield, eliminated one group of workers and hired another.

Mrs. Borden explained, "My father was so well thought of that he was the last of the Irishmen to be fired," she said rolling her eyes. "It was a fine gesture, but a hollow honor. It certainly didn't give much solace to the family of a skilled worker with no prospects for another job." She sighed. "Since I couldn't help them from way up in Beverly, my folks along with Kathleen, left the *Land of Opportunity* and returned to County Clare to work on a Brit-owned farm."

Continuing her narrative, Mrs. Borden said, "When she was twenty-four and facing the ridicule associated with being an old maid in Ireland, Kathleen married a bachelor farmer in his thirties who owned his own small plot of land. She and Shamus McHale had two children, a daughter, Mary, who died at four from smallpox, and," directing her eyes toward her nephew, "Thomas, here."

When he didn't interrupt, she said, "Although she was never able to have more children, Kathleen found that being the wife of a farmer suited her. It was enough for her to perform the chores and guide her independent-minded son through his childhood, puberty and teen years." She shook her head. "At least that was true until her life changed dramatically when the bank foreclosed on Shamus' land during the panic of 1896 when Thomas here was twenty-two. Soon thereafter, she and her husband along with Thomas emigrated back to the United States and returned to Boston."

"What does your father do for a living now?" I asked Thomas.

My new landlady intercepted the question and winking at me, said, "Like most no-good Irishmen, he sits in the pub all day drinking pints while his good wife works herself into an early grave."

Thomas let out a booming laugh, and I received an inkling of why people called him Boomer. Once he stopped laughing he said, "That's not really fair, Aunt Elizabeth. Some of us work really hard."

"Yes, *you* do, Thomas. That makes you the exception." She sighed. "As for your father, I suppose compared to most Irishmen, he's a pretty decent man."

Switching the narrative back to her own life, I noticed tears forming in Mrs. Borden's eyes. "My son, Sean, developed several fine retail businesses over the next twenty years in the towns around Boston. Unfortunately, he was also a sailing buff. The boat he and his wife were sailing capsized in a squall off Cape Cod. While pieces of the hull were found by fishermen, no one ever found the remainder of the boat or their bodies."

The old soul shuddered and continued. "A year to the dreadful day later, my granddaughter, Eileen, who was sixteen at the time she was orphaned, left me and all the grief I was groveling in. She was a sweet girl, beautiful and very bright," Mrs. Borden said, "but she was tired of living with her old grandmother and being forced to face all that loss on a daily basis. To help her move on, I bought this house that my son had left to her, helped her get into a college and for the next few years managed her financial affairs until she graduated."

"So, where is she now?" I asked.

"Tell him, Aunt Elizabeth," Thomas said with a sly grin.

"She graduated from Indiana University and married Conan O'Hara, a man she met there. They live in Chicago. He's in the milk business."

Thomas slapped his knee and began laughing as if he'd just been told a joke. "Eileen didn't marry no ordinary Mick. She got hitched to one of the few rich ones." He glanced at his aunt and grinned. "I don't want to wish her no trouble, but if the guy kicks, she can put her shoes under my bed anytime. She's beautiful and she'd have his money."

"Thomas, that's incestuous. She's your cousin."

"Aye! So she can have her own bed. Just so's she takes care of me, and I can sit in the pub all day and not be a sandhog no more."

Pretending to be disgusted, Mrs. Borden rose to her feet. "On that note, how about some tea for you gentlemen?"

I smiled and nodded.

"I'd rather ye had a pint, Aunt Elizabeth, but I know you ain't no barkeep."

"Nor will I ever be," she added with finality, neglecting to mention she had a bottle of whiskey in her cupboard for her nightly nip. "Now you boys talk while I'm fixing the tea."

"I'll be gettin' at it, Auntie." That was the first hint I had that Boomer's sudden appearance that day wasn't an accident.

"Do you know what kinda work me and the other boys does, John?" Admitting I didn't, he said, "Well, we work on the ground, in the ground and under the ground. We do everything that gives tall buildin's a strong foundation. Some boys dig in tunnels, but I ain't never done that. It's heavy bloomin' work crackin' rock and moving it, and dangerous, too. Boys gettin' hurt all the time losing arms and fingers and some dyin'. But, we make eight bucks a day, every day, rain or shine, and there ain't hardly any jobs around that pay that kinda big money to dumb Micks like us."

While he was taking a deep breath after his last statement, I tried to clarify something. "Thomas, I'm...."

"If you're gonna be one of the boys you got to call me Boomer. Or, as some do, shorten it to Boom." He gave a wave. "You were sayin'?"

"Stop calling me a Mick. I'm not Irish."

His face turned ashen. "You're an O'Malley, right? Then, what the bloomin' hell else can you be? A Rusky? A Polack?"

"I'm told I'm Scots-Irish."

"So you drink whiskey instead of stout, and your Da poked his lizard in the wrong hole. John O'Malley seems Irish enough to me." With that summary, he climbed off the dainty chair and sprawled onto the carpeted floor.

53

I never raised an eyebrow. By this time I'd been exposed to Boomer enough to expect anything. Also, his moving gave me a few moments to think about what he'd said. Since his lizard analogy described my philandering father perfectly, I couldn't quibble with Boomer's assessment. However, in my mind, my heritage was far more likely the result of a coupling between some bearded Viking and a Celtic lass centuries ago. I finally said, "I'm not new to America like you, Boomer. My aunt has traced our family back to the late sixteen hundreds in New Hampshire. She thinks some of my ancestors were in Maine even before that."

"So, you got a head start on some of the rest of us. Big pukin' deal! You're an Irishman."

"I'm not Catholic."

"Neither are most Irishmen, unless they're priests. We're not devout, for God's sake or our own sake. We go to the pub while the women get down on their knees and do the prayin'." He grinned up at me and gestured for me to join him on the floor. "I got a test for ye. I was goin' to give it to ye anyway, so now's as good a time as any. It'll prove if you're Irish or not, and it'll tell us both whether you're man enough to be one of the boys." When I hesitated, he said, "Well, come on, get down here, John, and give me a try." Since I was curious about what he had in mind, I joined him on the floor.

The first test occurred in a clearing between the dining room table and the couch. We were on our bellies and resting on our elbows head to head. Each of our right hands were clasped against the other. I'd won a few of these tests of arm strength before, but always sitting up at a table, never lying on the floor. We did it three times. The first time Boomer said "go." The next two times I did. Not surprisingly, the person who got the jump and slammed the other's hand to the floor, won. And, of course, each time that happened to be the person who said "go." Even a non-Irishman could figure that one out. Still, Boomer was impressed.

"Now ye got to do it with your leg," he said. "The boys call it Indian wrestling."

With that introduction we rolled over onto our backs with our heads at opposite ends and our butts next to each other. Then, at the count of three we locked legs at the knee and attempted to throw the other person over onto his side. With the first clash, Boomer let out a mighty roar and practically tore my leg off at the groin. That brought a hardy laugh from Boomer and an angry Aunt Elizabeth racing from the kitchen yelling at us.

She started with Boomer. "Thomas," she hollered. "You get off my floor before you break something. If you were to break my antique lamp, I'd have to take an ax to you." That was the first time I ever considered the possibility that Mrs. Borden might be one and the same with her namesake. "And you, John. Just because my nephew doesn't have any sense, doesn't give you permission to forget you are a guest in my house. Mind your manners."

Properly chastised, both Boomer and I returned to our respective seats. Wiping the sweat from my cheeks and forehead with my sleeve, I grinned at Boomer. He returned my grin and made a display of placing his hands in his lap, sitting up straight on the tiny chair and trying to look serious. When Mrs. Borden strutted in moments later, she smirked at both of us, and we all had tea and biscuits.

By the time the afternoon ended, Boomer had explained exactly what was involved in caisson work. "They call us sandhogs, but we really should be called rockhogs. We're the boys that blast holes in the rocks so's the concrete guys can pour deep footings for tall buildings. You know the sayin', 'A house built on sand will never stand. A house built on rock will be straight as a cock.'"

"I never heard that before."

He laughed. "Why would ye? I just made it up."

What I learned of value before that afternoon ended, was Sullivan Construction Company had a contract for all the caisson work on a new ten-story office building in central Boston. Since Boomer was one of the lead men on his part of the project, he could influence the bosses as to who was hired to work on his crew. "Do you know why they call me Boomer?" he asked.

I was sure it was because he was so loud, but I didn't have the courage to say it. He didn't wait for me to answer, anyway. "It's because I'm the boy who sets the dynamite in place and detonates it. I make the explosives go *BOOM*. Boomer! You got it?"

"I got it," I said, even though I was sure my first guess would have been right, also.

"Tomorrow, ye'll be startin' with a shovel and a wheelbarrow hauling rock from the hole to the pile for the steam-shovel to put in the wagons. Then, if you don't wear down too soon, in a few weeks you can go in the hole with me and haul rock to the elevator." He looked at me and smiled. "You ever been in a hundred-foot-deep hole, John?"

I shook my head.

"You ever drink a stout?"

"No."

"Then, I think ye got a lot of learnin' to do."

He asked Mrs. Borden for a paper and pencil. Instead, she handed him a pen and pointed to an ink bottle on the secretary. "You don't have a pencil, Auntie?"

"I do somewhere, but this should do fine." He smiled and began scribbling on a sheet of paper as Mrs. Borden looked over his shoulder with a horrified look on her face. When she couldn't contain herself any longer, she said, "Thomas, your writing is terrible."

"I don't need to be no Keats," he growled. "I'm just a dumb sandhog."

She put her hands on her hips and huffed. "At least you could write down the directions clear enough so John can find the site."

"This is the best I can do," he shrugged. Winking at me, he said, "If John can't read 'em that's his problem." When he was finished, he went over the directions with the names and numbers of the streetcars I needed to take the next morning until he was sure I understood them. "Follow me notes and be there at six-thirty," he commanded. He glanced toward his aunt who was retreating toward the kitchen with the tray of dirty cups and plates. In a voice loud enough to annoy her, he said, "Writing don't mean shite for a boy workin' down in the hole."

"I heard that, Thomas," his aunt said sticking her head around the corner and glowering at him for his language choice.

"I'm just showin' the boy the ropes," he answered. Then, turning serious, he threw his arm around my shoulder. "I want the boys trustin' ye when we start at seven tomorrow." Then he gave me a squeeze and said emphatically, "When you're down in the hole, trust is everything."

At the door, he shook my hand without crushing it, and called to his aunt to tell her he was leaving. While I watched from the parlor, she came running and they embraced. Then he gave her a soft goodbye kiss on the forehead and left. Later in the quiet of my room, I realized I'd learned a lot about Boomer McHale just by the way he said goodbye.

Chapter 12

TIM O'MALLEY

One could surmise that having a nomadic sandhog for a grandfather might generate wild stories of misdeeds, drunken fits of rage and encounters with evil. But, that would be wrong. At least Grandpa never shared any of his dirty underwear with me. Furthermore, if my father, Mike, bares hidden scars from some of my grandfather's exploits, he, too, kept them to himself. Therefore, without being privy to these unshared facets of John O'Malley's personality, I accepted him as a man-god incarnate, perfect in every way. It was only natural then, that by the time I was old enough to realize no man could be as perfect as my grandfather, I was already under his spell and basking in the sunshine of a loving relationship with him. Thus, I disposed of any suspicions by packing them away in an unused portion of my brain where they were allowed to ferment until such time as I wanted to quench my thirst for a more well-rounded view of my grandfather's life. That day never came.

However, since he'd been dictating stories about Boomer McHale and his early relationship with my grandmother, I've often wondered why I'd waited so long before taking a wee nip from the underside of his past. Nothing I've learned so far would have any negative effect on my love for him. In fact, it's opened my eyes to the fact that we have even more in common than I ever realized. Since Marie's death I've been running away from life instead of facing it. Now, just learning my grandfather ran away from his family at sixteen and lived a decent and happy life gives me hope. I'm forty for God's sake. I should be able to cope, and I am trying harder. At least I can see light where only a few months ago all I could see was darkness.

Still, it's complicated. My father is using booze to deal with the death of his marriage, and it's affecting his relationship with his father and me. I think it's a coward's way to survive, but who am I to get up in arms about it. After all, I'm still depressed over Marie's death, and my own son doesn't seem to respect me. So, while no man's future is ever clear, I just hope my son will eventually embrace me again. What he doesn't understand is I can't just reshuffle the deck and play another hand.

Chapter 13

Tim O'Malley

Since I've given the tape recorder to Grandpa O'Malley, I've been straining my brain to recall any incident from our shared past to which he can add his insight and get on a cassette tape. Not surprisingly, when we hit on one, we both share in the joy of the remembrance.

The earliest entry involving me occurred when I was a child of five. We were visiting my grandparents at their apartment in Chicago when they decided to go to Sears Roebuck. While my memory of the event is vague and hazy, I do remember sitting on the front bench seat straddling the floor shift of his new green '41 Ford.

With Grandpa driving and Grandma on my right, we set off on a journey from their four-family apartment on the corner of 82nd and South Park in South Chicago to the store on 63rd Street. "Tim, which direction are we heading?" Grandpa asked me casually.

I shaded my eyes with a hand to keep the glare of the morning sun from burning my eyes. "East," I answered.

Patting my knee, he said, "That's very good, Tim." Grandma added her approval by pulling me toward her with the hand she had draped around my shoulder.

Later, he turned left and asked me for the new direction. "North," I hollered.

"Excellent." Grandpa exclaimed. "You're a very bright young man." Another pat on the knee. Another hug. At the next corner, he turned left again.

"Now."

"West."

A right turn.

"North."

And he continued zig-zagging his way to Sears until Grandma tired of the game. "John, you're making me dizzy."

"Sorry, Flo. But we've a young genius in the car, and we ought to test him 'till he misses." Then he patted my leg once again and promised, "Chicago streets are on a grid, Tim. Some day you and I will go out in the fields or the woods to see if your compass works as well there. I believe it will."

I'm not sure whether Grandpa intended the trip as a teaching moment, or if the test came about spontaneously. What I do know is the result was a great confidence builder for me. I'm hardly ever lost, and on the rare occasion when I am, it's never long before I find my way.

Grandpa's next test came when I was ten after my grandparents moved to rural western Michigan. Back then following the war, my father only got two weeks of vacation and much to my mother's displeasure, one was always spent with her in-laws. This meant most days she would keep her mother-in-law company while the men-folk went out and played.

On one particular warm sunny day, my father, Mike, and I accompanied Grandpa O'Malley on a trout fishing expedition into the legendary Baldwin Swamp. The trip was memorable for two reasons. First, my grandfather treed a porcupine, the first I'd ever seen, and poked it with the end of his fishing pole to make it hiss. Second, he insisted I guide the party on the two mile walk back through the forest from the creeks where we fished to the place where we parked the car.

How does a ten-year old find his way out of a dense woods without an actual compass following paths and streams he'd never seen before? I'm sure the answer lies deep in my DNA. Certainly these were not learned skills since my only training occurred in the Ford five years before. The only plausible answer is my Grandpa O'Malley planted the seeds of confidence and observation on that earlier occasion so that when the time came to perform, I believed in my ability to find my way out.

Since Marie died, I'm facing an important test. If Grandpa's lessons have any relevance in my current setting, believing in myself will once again help me find the right path out.

This afternoon was so bright and sunny, I decided to leave my latest project at work half done and visit Grandpa at the home. So around three, I slipped into my Mercury Marquis and began navigating my way to pay Grandpa a visit. Heading west on Fifteenth Avenue, I turned north onto Eleventh Street. At the Illinois Central tracks that crossed Eleventh street, a few cars were stopped for a train. I slowed and eventually took a place behind a blue Buick. Since I wasn't in a rush to my destination, instead of cursing the wait as I typically would, I glanced at the Rockford Standard Furniture Company building on my left. Suddenly on an impulse, I steered the vehicle into the empty left lane, turned onto the street before the tracks and drove it into the company parking lot. Tucking in my shirt, I ran my hand through my hair and walked inside to chat with the new owner of the place, a friend I'd known since high school. Twenty minutes later, I had a new advertising client for the agency. Instead of cutting my trip short and returning to the office to share my find with my partners, I decided to savor my success, share it with my grandfather and impress my associates in the morning.

After hopping back into the Mercury, I ducked into the one-way traffic on Ninth, drove under the railroad viaduct and reached Charles Street. From there, I took a right onto Longwood, curled around Sinissippi Park on North Second and crossed the Rock River at the Auburn Street bridge. From there I wound through an established residential neighborhood, found Main and took it north to where Grandpa lived in an upscale nursing home. Although I'd traveled all these streets before at one time or another, the map I carried in my head helped hasten my journey to visit the man who'd once proclaimed me a geographical genius.

As I was entering the lobby of the large two-story building, I recalled a one-week visit with my grandparents during their later years when they lived in Montague, Michigan near the western shore of the great lake by the same name. This was their second stint in that part of the state. After the Second World War, my grandfather had taken a superintendent's job building a power-house in the Ludington area, and they had lived in Pentwater. In fact, that was the place they were living when I'd led our fishing party out of the Baldwin Swamp.

In 1951, I was just fifteen and learning to drive. I had my learner's permit and few skills. True, my dad had shown me the rudiments of starting his new Nash, braking it and shifting with the clutch, but he would never let me drive on the city streets and only once did he take me out on a dusty, deserted gravel road to practice while he sat next to me in the *death seat.*

Meanwhile, my fifteen-year-old friends were illegally driving all over town without an anxious adult by their sides. Quite realistically, I feared my inability to drive a car during that era would erase my status as an athlete and banish me to a teenage hell where I had no wheels, no friends and no confidence that using my fists would quiet the derisive barbs of those who taunted me.

Worse, my father, Mike, who'd grown up in an ancient era where horse and buggies still competed with street cars and a few Model T Fords, had little sympathy for my plight. In his mind, cars carried breadwinners to work or were used by the women-folk on Saturdays to run errands when the man of the house was home from the factory, the office, or in my father's case, a day driving from place to place in an attempt to sell factory supplies. They were definitely not toys to be played with by fuzzy-cheeked youths who might race them, crash them, or worse, entice a young female into the back seat of one and be forced to marry at a young age.

What I've learned as an adult is grandfathers are not burdened by the restrictions of parenting. They view their grandchild as a kindred spirit who has been tormented by a parent far too strict and far too stern. In my case, I think Grandpa O'Malley viewed me as a child deprived of youth's many pleasures and determined it was his God-given duty to remedy the situation. In short, even if I were the most unworthy adolescent, I should be spoiled rotten and given a long leash so I could flower into the brilliant adult my grandfather instinctively knew hid within my gangly frame. While I'll never know if Grandpa O'Malley saw me in that light, I chose to believe his actions seemed to suggest he did.

When I spent an extra week with my grandparents in Montague after my folks returned to Rockford that summer, I entered a celestial world where the sun revolved around me. My day began with a breakfast prepared by my doting grandmother which included all my favorites: stacks of pancakes smothered with butter and soaked with syrup, served with countless strips of crisp bacon. Never was I forced to eat the scrambled eggs, dry cereal or oatmeal that were the staples in my parents' home. Later each day, lunch and dinner were equally sumptuous and lovingly prepared to my specifications. Hovering over me with seconds and thirds, my grandmother was in ecstasy even when I ate too much, burped and pushed away from the table to play cribbage with my grandfather without removing my dishes or helping with the cleanup. The truth was, no matter what I did, she beamed over me like I'd just presented her with a gift as valuable as diamonds, gold or silver.

While I waited for the elevator that would carry me to Grandpa O'Malley's second floor room at Highland Manor, I also recalled the gift he gave me during that magical week. When he built their small one-story home in Montague with his own hands, he'd placed it on a two-acre lot on Cook Street. Behind the house lay a large vegetable garden where he raised enough produce to fill dozens of quart jars with tomatoes, tomato sauce, vegetables and more varieties of pickles than I knew existed. These were the residuals canned faithfully by my grandmother after the family had gorged itself at each meal with fresh vegetables and given away bushels to friends and neighbors.

The front of the house was flat, without shrubbery, and remarkable to me only because it had a long semi-circular gravel driveway. That was where I really learned to drive. Day after day, my grandfather encouraged me to take his Hudson, back it from the garage to the street and then drive it forward on the gravel, past the house until I again reached the street. There I would slip into reverse gear and repeat the trip backward. At times I'd stop and start going from first to neutral and back to get a feel for the clutch, and though I might grind it, or occasionally lurch, by the end of the week I became quite proficient.

"Do your remember when you taught me to drive when you lived in Montague?" I said after we'd hugged and Grandpa and I were seated next to the window in his room.

His eyes lit up and expressed the grin his mouth couldn't quite form. He shook his head back and forth and said, "Bad!" then after a struggle, he said, "Tree."

I knew he was referring to the recently planted small pine I backed over on one of my failed attempts to set the land speed record for driving in reverse. Fortunately, I hadn't been hurt nor had I damaged Grandpa's Hudson, but the sapling was reduced to kindling. "I'm sorry," I said, for the twenty-first time which was the approximate number of discussions we'd had on the subject since he'd arrived in Rockford.

"Okay." He laughed, pointed at me and turned palms up. "No... one died." Then he ended the discussion by stating he'd planted a new tree.

"And later, you knocked it down while you were backing out of the drive," I said.

That brought another laugh. After which, he added an episode to the story which was new to me. As he struggled with the sentence, I repeated each word to make sure I understood. "You wouldn't let me drive in the road because if I got hurt, you'd die?"

"Yes...Flo...kill me!" He made the sign of slitting his throat and pointed to himself.

Then he placed the back of his folded hands against his cheek and smiled like an adoring grandmother might and attempted to say "precious." It came out with three syllables, "pres-ci-ous," but I knew what he meant.

The subject terminated when he tossed me a crooked grin and shook his head. "Good dir-ec-tions. Ve-ry bad driv-er."

I laughed and decided to write that up and include it with all the other stuff he had recorded. It's the small gems from the distant past that creep from his brain onto his tongue and into the mic that are already making his story a classic, my visits memorable and keep me coming back to see him. Truly, each gem has a way of illuminating his spirit and showing his love. Even though his body is breaking down, I know the old sandhog will never give in. I see it when he leaves his wheelchair, shakes off my helping hand and walks haltingly to the table by the window where we usually sit. Most of all I hear it in his speech. While he has never been and certainly never will be an orator, Grandpa O'Malley's speech has been improving with each visit.

After Grandma O'Malley passed away and Marie died and before his last stroke, Grandpa insisted on continuing to live alone in his small apartment across the tracks from Rockford Country Club. While he probably should have had someone with him at all times, he refused to move back with my father or move to a nursing home. He felt the home was too expensive and Dad should be worrying about my mother, not him.

Of course, Grandpa, as well as Claire and I, never considered his living with us. We were in grief, and had our hands full with Michael. To compensate, we visited him on Sundays after church, and packed him into the car and had him over for dinner on many occasions.

The thing about Grandpa was he always expressed such pleasure at being with us and gave so much of himself when we were together, we never considered his visits a burden. I still remember the first time we saw him after his stroke. All he could do at first was make a few unintelligible sounds. What words he tried were garbled, and when we couldn't decipher them he gave up in frustration. After resorting to gestures, pointing and a scribbled word or two, he quickly learned to sprinkle his failed sentences with what became his favorite all purpose word, *shit*. When nothing else worked, he'd fall back on it to get his point across. I never knew the word had so many meanings.

With a lot of effort, his speech improved over time. Now, after his second stroke, he's retraining himself all over again. No one can ever call Grandpa a quitter. He just doesn't understand the word. Even now when he can't see either, I imagine he spends his days talking out loud to himself or anyone else who enters his unseen world. In fact, I'll bet anything, he's chatting up his nurse, Annabelle, every time he practices his steps, and I'll bet big money he'll never quit until he's boxed up and shipped off to his next destination. God, why didn't I inherit his fortitude.

When I visited today, as so often happens, our conversation turns to the topic of fishing. At times he struggles to relate the details of fishing experiences that occurred back when he lived in the East long before I was born. I think he might even be thinking he's talking with my father, who unlike me, can relate to the people and the area where the events occurred. I don't care because he seems to receive joy from repeating his tales, just as my father enjoys giving hole by hole accounts of golf rounds from the past on courses I've never seen. Since apples never fall far from the tree, I'm sure I'll one day be regaling my son, Michael, with some passion of mine–if I ever find one.

When Grandpa stops struggling with his words to catch his breath, I ask, "Do you remember the day I came back to your house in Michigan with the dogfish?"

He chuckles. "Yeah, shit fish." That comes out quite clearly.

"Grandpa, I was so proud of those fish. I was only eleven. They were the biggest I'd ever caught, and you threw them in the garbage!"

"Sor-ry." He shook his head. "Flo gave me hell."

"Since you gave me a lot of freedom when I visited you, I'd walked the mile or so to the White River that day. Like every other day during that visit, I carried my pole, small tackle box and a can of worms." I touched his arm and spoke even more succinctly. "I liked the fact that you trusted me."

He grinned. "Good at dir-ec-tions."

"When I reached the river, instead of fishing for sunfish off the steelhead platforms that stuck out into the river, I climbed up the embankment, crossed over the railroad tracks and saw a slough I never knew existed. I was so excited to try my luck in that new spot, I slid down the steep grade and tossed a worm into the water. Moments later a fish hit it hard."

"Shit fish!"

"I didn't know that then, I just knew I had a big fish on my line. So, instead of horsing it in, I just hung on until I wore it out. When I first saw it, I thought it was a bass or a pike, but I soon realized an eighteen-inch chartreuse colored fish with a dorsal fin that connected with a rounded tail was neither. Still, I was thrilled and strung the fish on my stringer and tied it up to the trunk of a sapling at the water's edge. Over the next hour I caught two more." Then I asked, "Do you remember the rest of the story, Grandpa?"

"Shit fish," he said again.

I laughed. "I then decided to take a short cut and walk the forbidden railroad tracks back to your house hoping I wouldn't be hit by the diesel engine hauling filled boxcars from Muskegon to Ludington where the car ferries carried them across Lake Michigan to Milwaukee.

"It was tough going, Grandpa. The fish were heavy, and I alternately dragged them over the ties or tossed them over my shoulder and let the slimy creatures slap against my butt. When I got back to your house, I was exhausted and stunk. That's when Grandma made me shed my outer clothes and escorted me to the shower, and you threw my fish into the garbage can, stringer and all. I cried when I found out. I expected to eat them for dinner."

"Dumb me," he said or "dummy," I'm not sure which. Suddenly, he had tears in his vacant eyes. I stood up and hugged him.

"You didn't understand how much those fish meant to me, did you?"

He shook his head. Then his smile returned and he repeated "shit fish," one more time, and I brought up another old memory from my youth. "Do you remember when you taught me how you caught crows with a fishing pole?"

His smile and nod told me he did.

No one ever believes me when I tell about my grandfather's war with the crows that scratched around in his garden and ripped up his seedling vegetable plants. He was probably angry enough with the large black birds to haul out his shotgun and rid himself of their aggravation, but he lived within the city limits, and he had neighbors bordering his property. That's when he devised his plan to fish for them.

The summer of my driving lessons just happened to coincide with the peak season for crow fishing. I'm not sure whether his whimsy was strictly a tactical maneuver in his war with the birds or an attempt to amuse me. I do know it was a singular experience watching a grown man holding a fishing pole with a large, black bird attempting to fly while tethered to the end of a fish line.

His plan was ingenious. He'd run off enough monofilament to lay a line through his screen porch door out into the garden. There, he'd make a noose, circle it in a bare area among the small plants and seed the center of it with corn. Then, moving the thirty or so feet back to my vantage point inside the screen porch, he'd take up the slack in the line by my side and wait for a crow to begin feeding. When a crow tramped anywhere near the noose, he'd yank the pole. That triggered one of two happenings. Typically the wily crow avoided the noose forcing Grandpa O'Malley to reset the trap. However, once in awhile, a giant bird would get caught. That was my grandpa's signal to reel it in causing the air to be filled with sights and sounds I'd never heard before or since. After much swooping and cawing, he'd bring the startled bird to the ground. I'm not sure what my grandfather would have done with the bird if I hadn't been there watching, but on the day I saw all this happen, he reeled the crow to the last feral on the pole, scolded it with a finger and cut it loose with a warning never to return to his garden.

"And, that's how you catch a crow," he said to me like a teacher preparing me for an actual real life final exam.

When I finished my reverie, I asked him again, "Grandpa, you do remember catching crows, don't you?"

He nodded and grunted, "Shitbirds."

Before I left, I brought up a family fishing story, many times recounted, that occurred a few years back when Michael was a young teenager and Grandpa was recovering from his first stroke. On one of our family visits following church, Michael and I were chatting with Grandpa while Claire was cleaning up the filthy conditions she found in the kitchen after a week of Grandpa's sight-impaired cooking. At some point I asked, "Grandpa, how would you like to go fishing with Michael and me in my new boat?"

"Shoorer," he said, flashing his widest half-smile.

The moment the words left my lips my son began vigorously shaking his head. Since I'd already planned to fish with Michael for walleyed pike in the fast water below the Rockton Dam, the added burden of getting an eighty-nine-year old stroke victim into and out of a boat at a makeshift landing and baiting his hook because he was blind took away some of the luster. Still, I give him credit. Michael didn't say a word, and the next weekend I trailed the boat to a landing, and we did fish below the dam.

We caught a few smallish walleyes, too, and Grandpa hooked a channel catfish and reeled it in to the edge of the boat like a pro before Michael netted it. When we finally packed up to leave the dam, we had a nice day's catch. Nothing overly exciting, but we weren't shut out as I had feared we might be.

The real excitement occurred after that when I pulled anchor and the motor wouldn't catch. I kept cranking with no results as the current caught the hull and we began drifting sideways down the channel. As we picked up speed, I glanced at Michael. He was on the edge of panic. Grandpa, on the other hand, was unaware and blissful. The speed of our runaway craft and the resultant wind blowing past his bald head like air over the wing of an airplane, brought a contented smile to his face.

I continued to crank with no results. While my motor had a habit of balking, it seldom took this long to kick in. The river narrowed, and we rounded a corner. I glanced ahead and to my horror realized the boat was rapidly bearing down on a newly fallen tree full of foliage that extended well out into the current. "Michael," I yelled when I knew a collision was inevitable. "Get down...no, get on the seat next to Grandpa and try to block the branches from hitting him." I pulled at the motor again and it sputtered and died. Furiously, I tried again and again until it caught, but it was too late. We had drifted into a forest of small branches.

I looked up and saw Grandpa. He was flailing his arms in an attempt to keep the branches from slapping at his face, body and arms. To my surprise he also had a grin plastered across his face.

With branches large and small surrounding us and the boat nestled prow-first into a notch made by the limbs, I peered through the dense foliage to assess the damages. While Michael was now in the prow trying to push us out of the forest and into the current with a paddle, Grandpa O'Malley sat motionless. Around him littering the floor of the boat lay an array of assorted leaves and twigs. In addition, he wore a mantle of small branches, had blood oozing from a small scratch on the side of his bald head and, of course, the old man was chuckling.

Once we were free of the tree, and backing out into the fast current, I asked a tentative question of both my passengers. "Is anyone hurt?"

My son gave me the circle sign to show he was fine.

My grandfather's response was equally swift and upbeat. With a hearty laugh, he said, "Shit, Tim. I thought we were goin' fishing, not hunting."

Today, after relating the story and hearing my grandfather laugh once more at his parting words from that long-ago trip, he looked up at me and asked, "Ca-ca-can we fish?" The nodding that followed was his attempt at encouraging me to take him once again. Still, with Michael away at college and the river water just below flood stage there was no way I would say "yes." I just couldn't handle him by myself.

"Your great-grandson, Michael, is away at college," I said.

"Annabelle, go," he said.

"Maybe sometime, Grandpa."

I watched as his chin dropped to his chest, and he sighed. Then he brightened. "Sometime, good."

After I left that day, I felt like a passing shower had just washed away the collected dust of a long hot summer. I actually felt joy. Joy for an old man who no matter how afflicted always looked forward to each new day and each new experience no matter how insignificant it might appear to someone living outside his failing body. I also experienced hope. I'd been given a valuable gift. I learned it is never too late to be healed.

While I was driving back to my house, I shed a sudden tear for my mother lingering in another nursing home with a brain that died before her heart. After spending a few hours with Grandpa, I was awestruck by the contrast.

Chapter 14

THE DIARY OF SANDHOG

The fateful streetcar ride the morning after I met Boomer McHale led me into a foreign world of crude, drunken, hard-working wild-men. What kept them from killing each other in their alien underground environment was the basic need for survival. When one was "down in the hole" where dynamite blasts, cave-ins and flying rocks were everyday hazards, a man without a buddy or two was a man to pity. Since serious injury was an everyday occurrence and premature mortality a given, any man who worked alone had to be a fool or entertaining thoughts of suicide.

My training started on top of the ground. I hauled small piles of debris that had spilled out of the steam shovel onto the ground and made a larger mound for the crane to scoop up and carry to a gigantic ever-rising mountain of rock. Early on, I'd heard the rock would end up as part of a new wharf in Boston Harbor, although I was kept so busy I never confirmed it. Then, a few days later I was lowered into the hole for the first time as a member of Boomer's crew, and although I was intimidated at first, I quickly got accustomed to working underground.

With daylight eighty feet above us, our small group of eight worked in a subterranean funnel surrounded by walls of solid rock. To make the excavation deeper and wider, drillers reamed out holes into the walls and floor for Boomer to fill with explosives. The rest of the crew, using picks and shovels, filled four-wheeled handcarts with the debris from the aftermath of the blasts. My job, besides shoveling rocks, was to push the filled cart to an open area and attach it to the hook of a steam-powered crane which raised it to the surface. Once it was topside, the cart was emptied by the crane operator and lowered back into the hole for the boys and me to refill.

Up on top, the crane operator added our rubble to that of five other squads of sandhogs who were also blasting and removing rock from five similar holes that would one day form the footings for the foundation of the building that would rise up into the Boston skyline. Ultimately, when the underground work was completed, there would be twelve such ninety-five-foot excavations in total.

One evening after our crew had been lifted to the surface in a tightly-packed cage by the crane operator, I decided to ask Pete, a co-worker, about the final resting place for the debris.

Pete grinned, "Aye, 'tis a mystery, ain't it, mate?"

Since Pete had been around long enough to know the answer, I figured it might take a couple of pints before he'd share his knowledge with the new boy. As it turned out I didn't even have to bribe him. As we walked side by side to the pub, he opened up to me. "While we're breakin' our backs in the hole, the boys up top haul the shite away in big horse-drawn carts."

"I know that, Pete. I filled a lot of those carts while I worked up top. I'm wondering where the shit goes?"

He smiled. "I won't lie to ye, John. They dump it into the harbor. One of these days our rubble will be a new ship dock."

When we arrived at the pub, I thanked him tangibly by buying him a stout. Since stout is the lubricant that loosens an Irishman's jaw, for the rest of the evening I received answers from Pete for questions I never asked.

While it was evident that Pete and the others knew a bit about working in the hole, it was Boomer McHale who was our guide into the underground world of the sandhog. I couldn't have been luckier being his friend, because even though Boom wasn't quite thirty, he was one of the most revered men in the whole brigade. He not only understood all the ins and outs of using dynamite to break rocks, but in addition, Boomer had an innate respect for the men who worked with him. Rather than just blasting away like some of his reckless counterparts, he approached digging through to bedrock as a team effort. While his above ground demeanor at times might belie his professionalism, Boomer McHale would never knowingly set off a charge that might bury one of his mates, put out an eye or otherwise maim a man with flying rock.

Boomer typically kept up a running commentary to keep us informed of his progress. He also kept track of "his boys" by shouting out questions and paying close attention to their answers. This afternoon was no exception. He had just set his charge when he immediately began a roll call of sorts. In a voice loud enough to break rock without the aid of explosives, he yelled at one of the newer guys, "Ian? Where are ye, lad?"

A voice well away from the stalagmite that soon would be demolished by Boomer's charge, yelled back, "Over 'ere, Boom."

He turned and spotted the sweat-coated, blackened-face of a gentle giant holding a pick. Boomer waved. "Aye, big fella. Now, you be stayin' there if you know what's good for ye."

Then, seeing his close buddy, Pat, shoveling the final bit of rubble from the last blast into a barrow-cart, he grinned. "Aye! Good boy, Patrick O'Connell. But unless you're wantin' a snoot full of this un, you'd better step back. And you, John," he pointed at me and growled, "Get that shite wagon back against the far wall. Ye don't want that thing jammin' up the way if we get a bad blow and need to run out of here fast."

When all seven members of his crew were accounted for, Boom lined us up well away from the blast area and told us to "Pull your bandanas over ye noses and mouths, bend over and 'old ye knees with your arses to the fire." When we were in position, he hollered, "Now, there's the smiles I like to see on yer faces." Then he lit the fuse and ran back to join us.

The explosion created a tumble of disengaged rock and a wind-gust that produced a fog of fine dust particles that settled on our hard-hats and clothing. When Boomer finally gave the signal to turn around, he grinned and pointed to the pile of rubble still smoldering like a pot of hot stew. Pulling out a cigarette, he said, "Let's have a smoke, boys, and let 'er cool down a bit. Then we'll have at 'er for the rest of the day."

By four-thirty I'd sent six barrow loads up to the surface, and we were about finished clearing the last of the debris when Boomer gave a sharp whistle for us to stop. "Listen up!" Wiping the dark sweat from his forehead and face, he said, "Boys, ye worked like fools today, and I'm proud of ye. I've set one more charge, and I guarantee you two dollars overtime if ye got enough in ye to clean it up before ye leave for the pub." He raised his hand to silence the murmur of our voices. "Or, ye can go to the pub right now. Your choice. Either way the first round's on me." He looked from one face to the next. "How ar'ye' votin'?"

I learned something important that afternoon from Boomer. While a drayman can work a horse till it drops, or a slavedriver whip his slave into submission, a foreman has to appeal to a workingman's heart to push him to his limit. Boomer must have instinctively known that, because we voted to a man to get the job done before the day was over.

Later at the pub, Boomer ordered stout all around for his boys. Mike McConnell, one of the married boys, had said his farewells at the site, but the remaining six of us had followed Boomer like the Pied Piper of Hamelin leading the rats to the sea. Unlike Mike, who was a bit older than the rest of us and had two boys and a girl waiting for him at home, another of the boys, Mickey Egan, was just getting used to married life and not yet weaned from going home with a pint.

A little guy for a sandhog, Mickey had met a lass named Eileen from County Cork on the ship from Dublin to New York. To relieve the tedium of the long journey, he and Eileen had paired up in steerage. However, as happens with many shipboard romances, neither ever expected their love to extend beyond the gangplank on that wharf in lower Manhattan.

Like many a young Irishman who'd come to America before him, Mickey had said goodbye to Eileen, toted his bag to Grand Central Station and caught the train to Boston to join up with a male cousin who offered to share his room until Mickey could find the best pubs and settle into a good Irishman's job. Similarly, Eileen was greeted at the pier by her older sister, Mary, and her new husband, Karl, who'd recently emigrated from Hamburg, Germany. After the two sisters' initial embrace, Eileen was whisked away to the Staten Island Ferry and a place in their apartment. Soon thereafter, she'd found work as a seamstress in a Manhattan sweatshop where she seldom saw the light of day or her new American home.

Between draws from his pint, Mickey laughed about the jobs available to the recent Irish immigrant. "I tried 'em all that first year," Mickey said. "I worked as a gandy laying railroad track, a stevie unloadin' ships, and then I found this job with you boys." He put his arm around Ian's big shoulder. "Some men get ahead in the world, some climb the ladder of success. I think we Irishmen are all headin' in the wrong direction digging our way down to hell."

Ian, the gentle giant, laughed and lifted Mickey over his head like a circus strongman. He then spun a few times in a makeshift dance before setting him feet first onto the roughhewn wooden floor. Clearing his head, Mickey laughed and said, "When the fight starts, I want Ian on my side of the fray."

"I'm no fighter," Ian said. "I'm a lover."

Boomer, who'd been unusually quiet to that point said, "Sure you are, Ian. Who'd 'ave ye? Maybe the donkey pullin' the junk cart. Aye! For sure it wouldn't be no lady."

Ian grinned. "No offense, Boom, but I don't see no geese flocking around you, neither. Maybe the fairies covered you with the wrong dust, and they be the only ones can stand ye."

"Ooh!" Mickey said, "If I had any money, I'd buy another round on that un."

"I'll buy," Boomer said. "Maybe another pint will put some brains in the big ox's head."

Patrick Murphy, who'd been silent to that point snarled and said, "Nothing like two brayin' jackasses to spoil a good drink. What I want to hear is how little Mickey here met up with his girl again?"

"At church, Patrick. I met her at church."

Boomer slapped his knee and roared, "Donkey shite. No self-respecting Irishman goes to church. You ain't been since ye got off the boat."

"I didn't say I was proud of it, but if I said I saw Eileen in church, you can bet it's true."

Ian threatened Boomer, "If my little buddy here says he saw her in church, then you better believe it."

"Aye," Boomer said. "Why am I doubtin' it? Hell, I can't even find the church."

"Anyway," Mickey said, "I was down in New York last year visitin' my Auntie and 'er husband for a weekend, and before she'd let me take the train back to Boston on Sunday, she made me go to Mass. So there I am sittin' on the hard pew and what do I see but my Eileen kneelin' and prayin' across the aisle a few rows in front of me. So when we're filin' out, I let her stay a bit ahead of me so she don't see me, and I can surprise her before she can get away without talking to me. When I'm out of the church, she's already standin' on the walk with her back to me. So I sneak up behind her and whisper, "I hope you were prayin' to the Virgin Mary for me."

Without turnin' around, she says, "I was, Mickey Egan, and she answered my prayer." Then she kissed me, and three weeks later we were married in front of the priest of that very same church."

"I bet ye ain't been back to the church since," Boomer said.

Patrick Murphy laughed. "Why would he, Boomer? He don't live in New York."

"Well said, Patrick me boy." Then Boomer stood up and said, "With that, I'm takin' me leave. I'm having a late supper with a beautiful lass." Starting toward the door, he turned and grinned, "Be bright and cheery-eyed in the mornin,' boys. We got a lot a rock to move."

"I'm got to get moving, too," I said springing to my feet. I wasn't really in a hurry. I'd only be going back to Mrs. Borden's for a bath, a warmed over meal and a night of dreaming about my lovely Flo. When I'd caught up with Boom, and we'd moved outside away from the others, I said, "I'm not so lucky as you, Boomer."

"Why's that, John McHale?"

"You got yourself a lass. Mine is in Maine."

"No, you be the only one with a lass." He placed a grimy arm around my shoulder and grinned. "Aye. 'Tis a special evening I'm havin' alright. I'm eatin' supper the same place as you with the same beautiful woman, me Auntie Elizabeth."

Seated side-by-side on the streetcar, I asked him, "Why is it, Boom, you don't have a wife or girlfriend?"

He winked, "What makes ye say that? I got a lass back in County Clare that wants me."

"But none in America."

"I don't want to cause no lass no sorrow. My lass may be missing me and a little sad at times being so far away across the sea from America, but it's a damn sight better than waitin' on the other side to join me in eternity. Ye see, John, I'm just one bad blow, one fast fuse, one flying rock from death. No faithful woman should have to be worrying about that every day when I leave for me job."

"So, why do we do it, Boomer?"

"In America, it's hard, dangerous work or the pub for an Irishman. Only a coward chooses the pub."

That night, like most nights, I wrote a letter to Florence before falling off to sleep. I told her about my day with the boys and how envious I was of Mickey for being able to fall asleep with his new wife at his side. I ended by asking Flo, *Do you love me enough to join me soon?*

The answer came back a week later when she ended her letter with, *John, I have thought about nothing else since your letter arrived. Yes, I love you enough to join you.*

All my love.

Flo

Two days later Mickey was crushed under an avalanche of flying stone that broke his spine. Considering what lie ahead for Mickey and Eileen, I began to wonder if she might not have been better off if she'd skipped Mass that fateful Sunday and never met up with Mickey again.

Chapter 15

THE DIARY OF A SANDHOG

In Mid-October of 1901 the caisson brigade completed all of the preliminary work for the Museum of Fine Arts Building on Huntington Avenue in Boston. With winter on the horizon and my savings approaching five hundred dollars, I tipped a final pint with Boomer, said goodbye to Mrs. Borden and took a streetcar to the huge South Station for the train trip back to Portsmouth. Once I was settled across the river in Kittery Point, I intended to dedicate myself to Florence, enjoy some hunting and fishing and rest up for an unknown job in a distant city the following spring. In addition, I looked forward to becoming reacquainted with Mr. and Mrs. Ferland and basking within the only positive family environment I'd ever known. Getting married on Saturday, the sixteenth of November wasn't part of my plan.

I was lying across my attic bed with Flo locked in my arms. We were whispering so as not to wake her parents when we talked about our promise to one another. While my passion for her played a key role in asking for her hand, other factors weighed heavily in my decision. I'd learned a lot about myself after six months as a sandhog, and one was the feeling of loss being separated from Florence. Although my job was a dangerous one, I could easily embrace the risks because of the good pay, the physical labor involved and the camaraderie of the boys. What I couldn't handle was the nagging emptiness. While I'd grown to love Mrs. Borden, her company was no match for the excitement I felt being with my Flo.

Still, as much as I wanted her with me, I had reservations about a marriage. For one thing, like Boomer, I wasn't sure Flo should be worrying about me each day when I left for the job. What if it were my mangled body instead of Mickey's being lifted to the surface for an uncertain future. Should I subject Flo to that terror or have her fearing the prospect of one day living with a one-armed or one-legged or one-eyed husband, or even worse widowhood?

In addition, there was the nomadic lifestyle I had yet to experience. Each season I could be moving to a new job in a distant city and hauling her along or staying apart for long periods of time. Heck, my Flo had never been outside of southern Maine or the small piece of New Hampshire that touched the Atlantic. How would she fill the long twelve-hour work days in rough cities like New York or out west in Chicago or St. Louis?

On the other hand, as we lay intertwined on that single bed, I only entertained these thoughts, I never spoke them. The warmth of her body against mine and the kisses that flowed between us seemed to outweigh any pain I might eventually cause her. Selfishly, I needed her and wanted her now, in our own apartment, because the odds of my finding another rooming house in another city with a hostess as sweet as old Mrs. Borden were astronomical. Since I had no desire to mimic the other boys who pickled themselves nightly at the pub to fill their off-work hours, I saw in Flo the balm that would free me from that empty existence.

"Do you still want to marry me?" I asked suddenly.

"Yes," she answered without hesitating.

"It's going to be tough..." and I went on to explain the pitfalls of hooking up with the likes of me.

"Oh, shut up, John O'Malley. I've heard enough." Then she rolled over, held me to her and all thoughts but pleasure left my brain.

The next morning while Mrs. Ferland was making my breakfast, Mr. Ferland invited me to go rabbit hunting. When I accepted, he patted my back, put on his hunting jacket and left the house to hook Maybelle up to the buggy. Meanwhile, I took my time over breakfast before trudging the stairs and kissing Flo awake. My parting took a bit longer than planned, so when I finally did join Mr. Ferland in the yard, he and Maybelle were both anxiously pawing the ground to get going.

After I climbed up into the buggy, Mr Ferland followed suit, sat down on the board next to me and grabbed the reins. Between us, two shotguns stood upright leaning against the seat. A box of ammunition lay by our feet. Perhaps it was the lingering glow of the previous night, or maybe it was the symbolism of the shotguns resting near his hand, but for whatever reason, I decided to enhance the hunting trip by professing my love for his daughter and formally asking for her hand in marriage.

While we traveled to the Ebson farm where Mr. Ferland had an open invitation to hunt, I practiced the words I would use. Hopefully, during the silence I created while committing my speech to memory, Mr. Ferland's thoughts were elsewhere. With luck he was focused on driving Maybelle, or on Homer, the beagle who always accompanied us on rabbit hunting forays, and not concocting an antidote to stifle my proposal. While I knew he liked me and cared about me, I wasn't at all sure he wanted his daughter marrying a sandhog. At one point, I peeked at him and felt relief. None of my concerns registered on his countenance. By the look of contentment on his face, I surmised he was merely enjoying the crisp fall air, the feel of the reins and the sound of Maybelle's hooves clip-clopping on the macadam.

To be safe, I returned to my task and ran through what I wanted to say one last time. When I felt fully prepared, we were traveling among the trees on the long narrow dirt road that ended at the Ebson farmhouse. With the homestead in view, instead of sharing the fruits of my practice, I blurted out, "Mr. Ferland, Florence and I want to be married. Will you give us your blessing?"

He relaxed the reins, turned and studied my face. "So, you're asking permission to marry my only daughter?"

"Yes," I said, surprised that the word *yes* came out like loose gravel.

"And, where will you live?"

"I'm not sure, yet, sir. I know I can work on the caisson crew back in Boston for the Mother Church Extension at the Christian Science Church on Massachusetts Avenue in the spring, because my friend, Boom...Thomas will want me on his crew. I also have my name in for a large job with a company in Baltimore that pays more money than Sullivan and has work lined up for several years. If I get that, we'll live there."

I flashed a questioning smile. For the moment, my voice sounded confident and the quaver had disappeared.

"So, John, am I to understand you want me to give you permission to drag my only child off to some unknown location in some big city where you have no confirmed job to support her? Is that what you're telling me?"

I nodded, adding meekly, "But, not 'til spring, sir. I was kind of hoping to stay with you and Mrs. Ferland until then, have a spring wedding and then move."

His voice seemed to get louder. "Oh, so you want to move back with my wife and me, put off enjoying married bliss until spring and then receive my blessing to tear my daughter away from us, live who knows where in some God-forsaken large city and leave my wife and I with nothing in return but our love for each other."

I rubbed the back of my hand over my forehead. "That's not quite the way I see it, sir, but it probably looks that way to you."

Suddenly his face got red, and he looked as if he was about to explode. "I should hope I'm entitled to my opinion." Then he did explode. Only it was not into a fury, but an uncontrollable convulsion of laughter. Between spasms, he said, "It looks to me like I'm not losing a daughter. I'm gaining a son." With that he placed the reigns in his left hand and hugged me with his free arm. "Sorry to be so hard on you, John! Nothing could make me happier."

That whole day we didn't shoot one rabbit, but, in my mind, it would be the most productive hunting trip I'd ever experience in my life.

After I received Mr. Ferland's blessing, the women took over the project and gave it life. Instead of a spring wedding that might conflict with my work schedule if I were called back to Boston or Baltimore prematurely, Mrs. Ferland and Flo decided to have it earlier. After considering a mid-winter ceremony and dismissing it because of the probability of bad weather, they decided on the Saturday before Christmas. However, that date conflicted with a pageant at the Congregational Church, so they settled on Saturday, November sixteen. Since the date was earlier as opposed to later, Florence was elated. Personally, I didn't much care when it was held just as long as Flo and I were married by the time I would leave Kittery Point the following spring.

As the date for the wedding approached, Flo and her mother entered a frenzy of activity. Since Flo had decided to be married in her mother's wedding dress, there were numerous fittings and many alterations until it was perfect. In addition, they developed a guest list, wrote out invitations and planned a reception to follow the service. Plus, they spent many hours consulting with the Congregational minister.

Once Flo had asked her best friend, Prudence Hartnett, who now lived in Concord, Massachusetts, to be her Maid of Honor, a new round of activity began. Using the mail, they attempted to coordinate each other's gowns and accessories to show off the best features of Flo's tall willowy figure and Prudy's short buxom one.

During the first week of planning and preparation, Mrs. Ferland thought it wise to bring me into the process. "Will you be contacting your father and brother or should we just send them an invitation?"

The question caught me by surprise. "Why would you invite them?" I asked. "They won't come anyway. In fact, I don't even want to give them the satisfaction of getting an invitation."

She looked startled. "I knew there was some friction, but wouldn't a father want to meet his son's bride and witness the wedding?"

Knowing my lecherous father's taste for beautiful women, I was sure he'd be only too happy to get to know Flo. Still, I told her, "I doubt he would."

She sighed. "So your brother isn't going to be your Best Man, either?"

Thinking I'd rather have the Devil himself than my brother, I grimaced. "Good Lord, no!"

She responded, "I'm certainly glad Congregationalists' families get along better than that."

To which I shrugged and wisely said nothing.

"So, who is going to be your Best Man?" she asked. "Another relative?"

Since no one ever told me about any other male relatives, and I'd never thought about a Best Man, I shrugged again. In fact, I did a lot of shrugging that morning because I didn't have the slightest idea about much of anything.

"How about Mr. Ferland?" I suggested.

"Don't be silly. How can he be the Best Man at the same time he's giving his daughter away?" I could tell the Best Man problem was getting to her, because she left the room shaking her head. A few moments later she returned. "Who's your best friend, John?"

Without hesitating, I hollered out, "Boomer."

She raised her hands to her face so I wasn't sure whether she was laughing or in shock. "Boomer?" she repeated. "Is that a real person?"

"Yes, sort of...I mean, his real name is Thomas, Thomas McHale. He lives in Boston. I worked with him."

"Thomas is a nice name," she said. "Why don't you ask him to be your Best Man?"

Just the thought of Boomer in a Protestant church, improbably sober and in formal dress sent me toward the stairs feeling perplexed. "Maybe I will ask him," I said to Mrs. Ferland. God help us all, I thought to myself.

The next day, I borrowed Maybelle and the buggy and drove to Portsmouth because I'd heard about the new long distance telephone line that just opened between Portsmouth and Boston. Although a telegram would probably be a more reliable method for getting a message to Mrs. Borden and eventually Boomer, I was anxious to try it out. In addition to its novelty, I was drawn to the telephone because it gave me an opportunity to actually hear the voice of my sweet old former landlady. As good fortune would have it, prior to my leaving, Mrs. Borden had a phone installed, and she'd given me her number. Although few others, including her nephew, had the resources to afford the outrageous three dollar per month charge, she deemed it a fine investment to have the new technology in her home. Not only were the voices of her world at her fingertips, but Mrs. Borden would feel safe knowing that in an emergency she could call Mrs. Florence Baker, who also was similarly equipped, without having to walk the three doors to her home at 2104 Oxford Street.

I eventually found the American Telephone & Telegraph Company office where I gave the young attendant the number Mrs. Borden had given to me. He then placed the call. Hearing her voice crackling through the wire sent a chill down my spine.

When she realized who was calling, she asked tentatively, "Is something wrong, John?"

"Not unless getting married is a sin."

Never without a quick comeback, she answered, "If I know my Bible, I believe marriage can keep you *from* sinning." Her next words were tainted by static. When I said I hadn't heard what she'd said, she repeated them and the message came through loud and clear. "You have my congratulations, John. Your Florence is a fortunate woman."

Overcome by her compliment, I descended into meaningless small talk. Finally I said, "I want Thomas to be my Best Man."

She laughed. "Now that might be a sin. That boy is all Irish, you know. I'd have to scour the pubs to find him."

"He's my best friend," I stated.

"He's a good boy, he is. I'll find him and give him the message even if I have to take a carriage to his apartment and leave a note for him. What is your telephone number?"

I explained that the distance between the Ferland's home and the exchange was many miles so I suggested Boomer send his return message by telegram.

"When is the wedding?" she asked.

"November the sixteenth."

"That's certainly very soon."

"I know. It's not entirely my idea."

"Oh, my!" Then the telephone went dead. At that point I questioned my decision to call Mrs. Borden on the telephone. To avoid any misunderstanding, perhaps instead I should have sent Boomer a telegram.

Boomer arrived on schedule the night before the wedding, and Maybelle and I were at the Portsmouth train station to pick him up and transport him to the Atlantic Inn in Kittery. The first thing I noticed when he came staggering down the platform was he had no valise. The second surprise occurred when he grabbed onto me and smothered me with a hug. His breath and clothes carried the aroma of an alcohol-vomit mixture that gagged me and almost caused me to retch. It was immediately apparent Boomer had found the club car on the train.

Although I was disgusted with him, I remained cool and asked, "Where's your luggage?"

The question brought a frown. "I dunno."

"Did you have it on the train?"

Another blank look. "I dunno."

I silently cursed my ability to ruin a perfectly fine wedding by selecting a Irishman for the Best Man.

Behind me, I was distracted by a voice with a Southern accent hollering in our direction. Turning my head, I sighted a Negro porter running up the platform toward us toting a black leather suitcase. He was sporting a wide grin. When he reached us, he placed the bag by Boomer's side and said to me, "Ah do believe Mr. McHale was so excited to see you, he rushed off without his bag."

I looked at Boomer. His glazed eyes and insipid expression told me he didn't have any idea what the man had just done for him. I admonished him. "Aren't you going to thank the kind gentleman for bringing your bag?"

"Than' you," he slurred.

I reached into my pocket for something tangible to give the porter, but he stopped me by saying, "No need, Sir. Ah'm happy to take care of Mr. McHale. He was overly generous on the trip."

Having seen Boomer in action many times, I knew the gratuities grew with each additional drink. "And over served, I see."

"My mistake, ah'm afraid." He glanced at my Best Man. Drool dripped from his chin. That brought concern to his dark face. "Mr. McHale was telling me all about the wedding. Surely he'll be fine by tomorrow."

When my face gave away my doubts, he said, "You have my best wishes, sir."

I wasn't sure whether he intended his words to apply to my wedding or Boomer's ability to fulfill his role in the ceremony, so I sighed and said, "It may be a long day."

After a hearty laugh, he studied Boomer and concurred. "Yes, sir. It might be."

The stream of travelers were flowing by us as a river flows by an island when all of a sudden Boomer's knees buckled, and he toppled forward. Fortunately, the porter caught him and steadied him before he fell on his face or landed in a heap on the wooden platform. Boomer allowed himself the luxury of the man's arms before his eyes flew open and he began separating himself from his savior. Noticing the crowd gawking at him, Boomer flashed a liquid smile, stood up straight and tall and patted the porter's back in appreciation. "Than' you," he said, again.

Before taking his leave and heading back to the train, the porter said, "It's been my pleasure, Mr. McHale."

He sounded surprisingly sincere.

We turned and joined the other travelers slowly streaming down the platform. One by one they peeled off, but not before looking back with amused smiles. All but one old bitty who intentionally frowned at the sight of Boomer and made some loud clucking sounds before moving on. I chalked her off as an irate temperance advocate.

On our way to the modest station, we trudged past the mail car, the coal tender and the hissing steam locomotive. At times, Boomer struggled to stay upright, but he never fell. Meanwhile, I carried his bag and tried not to breath through my nose and thus be asphyxiated by my Best Man's stink. When we reached the station, I held the door for him and followed his unsteady steps into the small waiting room.

When we eventually made it to the curb where I had tethered Maybelle to a hitching post, I helped Boomer place his foot on the steel step, boosted him into the buggy and prayed he wouldn't topple out onto the street before we reached the Atlantic Inn. He rode the whole way with his head laying against my shoulder.

"Thomas was quite tired after working all day and then riding the train," I told Florence and the Ferlands when I finally entered their living room. "He wanted to go right to the Inn so he could get a good night's sleep."

"We were hoping to meet the young man tonight and go over some of the details for tomorrow," Mrs. Ferland lamented.

"He was of the same mind, but insisted he wanted to make a better first impression." Trying not to show the dread I felt, I said cheerily, "I'll fetch him in the morning so you'll have plenty of time to get acquainted before the wedding."

That night I knelt by my bed and prayed. It was the first time since I was a child that I'd fallen to my knees. Never having had complete trust in a forgiving God, I thought my doing so might impress Him. In my prayer, I said, "Please God. If you can't help Boomer recover his composure in time for the wedding, please let him die in his sleep."

The next morning when Maybelle and I met him at the Inn, I was greatly relieved to discover my prayer had been answered. Not only had Boomer made it through the night, but he was well-groomed, smelled fine and had a guilty smile plastered across his face. "Aye, John. Top of the mornin' to ye. I was a bit out of sorts last night, I'm afraid."

"You were a definite trial, Boomer, but no hard feelings. I'm just glad you're here."

I drove him back to the Ferland's by way of the Haley Road so I'd have time to discuss the details of the day with him. Before the four o'clock service, we had to all get acquainted, have our rented formalwear fitted, and meet with the minister at the church to go over the details of the ceremony plus have a run through. In the process, his job was to impress the Ferlands, my Flo and the Maid of Honor, Prudy.

Gesturing at the curvy tree-lined dirt road and the now fallow fields, Boomer said, "Tis a fine land this Kittery. It reminds me of Ireland."

"I've never been to Ireland, but I've often thought it would be nice if there were a need for sandhogs in Kittery rather than the big cities."

"Aye, a pint would go down smoothly in a beautiful place like this."

His comment reminded me of a topic I'd neglected to discuss. "Boomer, these Congregationalists don't drink alcohol. The reception this evening will be food and punch, but no liquor, wine or ale."

I felt his eyes burning holes into the side of my face. If he'd been carrying a charge, I'm sure he would have set it off right then and blown both of us to kingdom come.

"And, ye didn't have the apples to warn me?"

"I wanted you for my Best Man so badly, I didn't want to take a chance you'd say no."

There was a period of silence before he shouted, "Stop the buggy!"

"Why?"

"I said, tighten them reins and stop."

Already familiar with Boomer's erratic temperament, I began to slow Maybelle. "If you want to leave, I'll take you back to the station," I said. "But, I won't let you off out here in the country."

He hadn't spoken by the time I reigned in the horse and stopped, so I fully expected him to be jumping from the buggy. When I turned to see what he was up to, he lunged at me with a big grin. "I ain't leavin' my pal. I'm just needin' a hug." With that he pulled me toward him.

Every time I'm with Boomer, I find out something new about him. Sometimes, like the previous day, it's disgusting. Other times like today, it can bring tears to my eyes.

With a mile to go before we reached the Ferland's, I brought up one last bit of information. "Boomer, for the rest of the week-end, you're going to be Thomas. I'll call you by your given name and introduce you to the locals the same way. When you return to Boston, you can be Boomer again, okay?"

His protest consisted of whimper. "Are ye embarrassed to call me Boomer?"

"No, but Boomer is what you do. Thomas is who you are."

"Aye, ye may be right, mate. Yesterday, on the train I was Boomer. Today, I'll be Thomas, because he's as dry as an old lady's....Thomas don't drink."

That afternoon the ceremony went off exactly as planned. Florence was gorgeous in her mother's wedding dress, Prudy looked beautiful and other than my voice quaking when I repeated my vows, I played my role well. Not to be outdone, Thomas could have been a deacon in the Congregational Church for all anyone would know. Albeit a handsome one with a ready smile and a sense of humor. He was quite unlike some of the dour attendees.

Around seven-thirty, when the last bit of food had been con-sumed, the wedding cake cut and eaten and the bouquet tossed and caught, Flo and I were ready to get away. Just then, a carriage rented for the occasion by a local dry goods merchant friend of the Ferlands showed up and the driver whisked us off to a fancy hotel in York Beach for our first night together as husband and wife. We ordered breakfast from room service at one the next afternoon.

Upon returning to Kittery, we learned that following the wedding, Thomas had entertained Prudy into the wee small hours of the morning. He'd hired a handsome cab to take her to her hotel, and according to Prudy's account, paid to keep the cab waiting until he was ready to return to the Atlantic Inn. I'm not sure how much of her story was fiction, because they were spotted having an early breakfast together at her hotel before they both left on the train for Boston. Later, when I tried to learn the facts, Boomer was uncharacteristically mum.

Chapter 16

The Diary of a Sandhog

Looking back on all those earning years, I realize our adult lives together were quite different from those of the boys I worked with. For example, Flo and I took vacations, a week in the spring and a week in the fall and sometimes more when I was between projects. Wherever we were living at the time, we'd always end up in Kittery Point. For Flo, Mike and myself those trips home were always the highlight of the year. Flo could pick up where she left off with her aunts and uncles, dozens of cousins and childhood friends. It was like heaven for her. Year after year she knew they'd all be there, because no one moved away and no one seemed to die. As her Aunt June once said, "If you're already in heaven, what is the advantage of dying?" She lived until she was ninety-seven.

While I enjoyed the women folk and especially their culinary accomplishments, I spent most of my time with the men. They were great folks. They'd take me fishing on the ocean and in the river, and if we were there in the fall, we'd hunt. So while Flo visited, for two whole weeks I got to do all the activities I enjoyed that the big cities didn't offer.

Kittery Point also became home for Mike. Although other than the year of the flu epidemic, he never spent extended amounts of time there. He admitted to me once that Kittery Point was the one place on earth where he felt at home. I understood that because my choice of life's work was tough on a kid growing up. We were always on the move. One year it was New York, the next it was Baltimore, and much later, East St. Louis. Every time I displaced him, he had to meet new people, go to new schools and get used to a new apartment neighborhood. Kittery gave him roots, a place with solid people, a home town. That's why he and his mother visited there for a couple of weeks every summer. He got to know his family, and when he was older, he, too, got to fish and hunt and even do some lobstering with his cousins and uncles and me. Those were joys a boy should experience, not the big city stuff he was forced to endure.

When Mike and I were talking a few years ago while visiting Sara and him in Rockford, he could still recall the big cod he caught one day out past the point. By contrast, when I asked if he remembered who beat him up in the alley behind our apartment in Baltimore or what started the fight, he went dumb. He didn't even remember the part where I beat the crap out of Sean Jamison's old man for letting his kid terrorize him. It was hard to believe the whole ugly affair had faded from his memory, but I was sure glad it had.

While some may think my vagabond way of life was hard on my wife and son, I don't know how I could have lived it much differently. Life was hard back then. One paid a big price to be a good provider, and I was certainly that. We had all the necessities, good food, thanks to Flo's great cooking skills, and a roof over our heads. Mike had a fielder's mitt and a couple of bats plus a saxophone and clarinet, and we had those two weeks in Kittery Point each year. So what if we were missing a few of the luxuries. Who needed them? In fact, I never could understand why any sane city person wanted to spend a fortune to flock to some fancy-pants resort close to the large city where they lived. I've lived in those cities, and I totally understand why they'd want to get away for awhile, but I've never understood why they'd want to dress up for dinner or play golf or play croquet on the lawn with a bunch of snooty people. Hell, I'll even bet if they went fishing, they'd have a guide bait their hooks and take off their fish. Where's the fun in that?

Still, I'll have to admit, all that uppity-uppity crap beats living here in Highland Manor with a bunch of old farts who flop in their wheelchairs in front of the TV and never get to do anything outside in the fresh air. Who wants to live in hell? No one does.

Chapter 17

JOHN O'MALLEY

I know it's August because they keep the windows shut and the air conditioning turned down so low I'm freezing to death. I sometimes wonder if there's a method to their madness. Maybe, if this old body was exposed to the sunlight and all the heat and mugginess, it might begin decomposing and stink up the place. After all, they keep cadavers cold don't they, and compared to my body there's not much difference. Come to think of it, I might be on to them. Judging by the way I'm treated around here, they may think I'm already a stiff. Except for Annabelle, of course. She's the one ray of sunshine who warms up the place.

Yesterday when she wheeled me down to lunch, instead of pushing me up to my usual table with another old guy who can't talk, she made me get out of the wheelchair and take her arm. Then, she marched me over to the table where two blurry old crones were chatting away and plopped me down between them at their four-top. While I was getting situated, the women stopped in mid-babble. I presumed they were giving me a smiley welcome. At least I didn't sense any resistance to my presence. I smiled back. Once they recognized my limitations, would they continue their friendly responses? Actually, I'm doing quite a bit better in the speech department since I've been talking into Tim's machine and Annabelle's begun working with me. Not only can I talk in understandable sentences sometimes, I also can say *shit* with perfect clarity to express my frustration or my surprise or how I feel as in "like shit." What a great all-purpose word for a blind-mute.

Actually, I learned the word early on working in the bowels of the earth with some of the world's toughest men. I only resurrected it to impress Tim and annoy Annabelle during our daily speech lessons. The reality is she's not the best speech teacher I ever had because she doesn't speak so well herself. She's got that soft Southern drawl that makes everything she says sound like black-eyed peas and chitlins. However, she's a realist. She knows that in order to understand what's going on in my head, she has to be able to read my scribble or understand what I say. The wonder is she cares enough about me to try to teach me new words. Even though Alice, the white woman, has been much nicer to me lately, I get the feeling she'd prefer peace and quiet.

Annabelle placed the napkin in my hand, and said, "Awl bet these ladies would like havin' a little male companionship. Right ladies? This is John."

The one on the left laughed. "Not many of those kind around here." Her voice tinkled like wind-chimes, so I made the assumption she was a skaggy-looking old stick. Then she said, "I'm Jenny, and this is Marion. She can't hear too well, so you'll have to talk loud."

I can hardly wait for her to find out I can't see and can barely speak.

Annabelle came to my rescue. "John's had a stroke and is still having a little trouble with his speech, so if one of you ladies would order for him when the waitress comes, he'd appreciate it. Right, John?" I turned toward her and nodded, so she said, "He wants the tuna salad sandwich, pear and cottage cheese and ice tea."

"Huh?" said the woman on the right.

Tinkles spoke up. "Marion is deafer than a post, but don't worry, I got it." Then she asked, "Doesn't he want some dessert?"

"Ice cream," I said. It sounded alright to me so I hope she wrote it correctly on the order sheet. Later, after Annabelle left, I found out she hadn't heard it right because they brought me chocolate pudding. Then again, maybe Jenny was the one with a deficit because I also got chicken salad on a croissant and Jello instead of what Annabelle had said to order for me. Anyway, by that time I didn't much care what I ate. I wanted Annabelle to get me out of there before I went nuts. How long was a guy supposed to listen to two old dolls screaming at each other about knitting mittens. Hell, I don't have any nieces that I've ever met, and even if I did, I sure wouldn't know how to knit them mittens.

The highlight of the day occurred after dinner when my son, Mike, showed up for the first time in a long while. It seems that after talking with Tim, he wants to tell stories into the machine like I am. If that's what it takes to keep him out of the tavern and coming around to see me, I'm all for it. I could give a rip what his motivation is. I just like having him around.

Chapter 18

JOHN O'MALLEY

By the time Annabelle came in this morning, I had dressed myself and was standing by the bed. When we first started walking lessons, this had been the goal. Get up, get dressed and go to the can by myself. After conquering those activities, we later expanded the goal to short walks up and down the hall and taking occasional meals in the dining room, and that's where we are now. Still, I want more. Not that I want to run a marathon or anything, but just in case some sexy lady about thirty years my junior wants to spend the rest of HER life with me, I'd be perfectly content if I were able to walk down a medium length church aisle.

It's not really that fantasy that has me itching to improve my speech. It's the frustration of not being able to be understood. Tim understands me, or so he says, and so does Annabelle. That's why whenever she has a moment, she works with me so I get better. She's no speech therapist like the babe I had after my last stroke, but she tries hard. She'll say a word or sometimes a short phrase, and I try to repeat it after her. We started with *please* and *thank you* and progressed to *good morning* and *how are you?"* Then we tried whole sentences like, *It's a beautiful day* and *The moon comes over the mountain*. However, I relearned "shit" all by myself one day because I was angry when she was too busy to work with me. That was quite an achievement at the time.

"How are you?" I said when she came in to take me to breakfast.

"Not so good."

I reached out and touched her forearm. "Was wron?" I need more practice on that phrase.

She eventually told me her TV set blew its tube and her two kids couldn't watch cartoons. She also said, "The old set's not worth fixin,' and we can't afford to buy a new one right now."

I said, "I'm sorry."

And she said, "No, I'm sorry to trouble you with my problems, Mr. O'Malley. I wouldn't have said anything if you hadn't asked me."

I was thinking that was kind of a dumb thing to say because what are friends for, but I didn't say it. Nor, did I tell her about the plan I just cooked up because I had to talk to my son first.

Fortunately, this afternoon he popped in to see me. Or, maybe I wasn't the main attraction because after a few pleasantries he went right to the microphone and began telling a story about his "uncle" Boomer. It was a new one for me, and I think Tim will get a kick out of it. Something about playing cribbage. Anyway, when he finished I took his arm and walked him over to the table holding the TV set I had brought from my apartment. Since I haven't had it on, I wasn't sure it still worked. I said to Mike, "Turn it on." His hesitation told me he was having a problem understanding. "On! On!" I repeated.

"You want to watch TV?"

"No. It works?" I'm not sure he understood exactly, but after a moment I saw screen-flashes and heard the rabbit ears scratching across the top of the set as he adjusted the picture. "It works good?" I asked.

"Yeah, but what difference does it make, Dad. You can't see it."

I wanted to tell him that it makes all the difference in the world, because I was giving the set to Annabelle, but saying that was beyond my ability. All I could say was "Annabelle nice. Give to her." I call it Indian talk.

Apparently I was getting better at this speaking thing than I realized, for he said, "You're giving your TV to the Negro aide?"

"No, Annabelle," I said.

"Did she ask you for it?"

"No!" I said emphatically. I was beginning to catch his drift, and I didn't like what I was hearing. I stamped my foot for emphasis. "No! No!"

There was a pause, then he said with a shrug of resignation in his voice. "Well, it's your TV." Next thing I know he's laughing. "Dad, you'd give the shirt off your back if it wasn't buttoned on. How are you going to get it to her house?"

"I dunno."

Then, despite all he had on his plate with his wife and such, he asked, "Do you suppose the office would give me her address so I could deliver it to her?"

"Shooer," I said and pointed somewhere in the vicinity of the table that held the phone. Actually, I wanted to kiss him except we didn't do that kind of thing. I'd always been afraid it might turn him into a pumpkin or a fairy princess or something like that. Instead I said, "Good son." He got that message, because he initiated a bear hug before he dialed the front desk.

Later, after he gave me another hug and prepared to leave, I heard him grunt and curse a few times. I'm certain he was hoisting the TV onto his shoulder. I also heard a clank as something hit the floor. "Damn rabbit ears," he hollered. With all the plugs and cords he was juggling on the trip to the car, I'm surprised that was all he'd said. Mike never did have a lot of patience.

Still, loaded down as he was, I heard him pause outside my doorway to answer an unknown questioner. "It's a gift for Annabelle."

That made me feel good all over.

When I woke up the next morning, my old heart was thumping so hard I could hear the beat in my ears. It's always been like that whenever I'm excited. It was early, but I didn't care. I wanted to be all dressed and finished with my bathroom chores by the time Annabelle arrived. When I'd accomplished what I set out to do, I edged over toward the window and sat in the chair.

While I couldn't see much but glare, I did manage to conjure up an idea of what an August morning in Rockford was like from my memories. Since it wasn't yet freezing from the air conditioning, I imagined the sun blazing down on me as I held a pole off the side of my grandson's fishing boat. All that imagining started my face to heat up and begin to sweat and cause a trickle to make a path down my cheek toward my chin. It's a good thing I didn't get a bite right then because I had to lay the pole down next to my chair so I could mop my face with my shirt sleeve. Golly, I thought. I never remembered hot sticky August mornings playing with my head like that before.

With all that fishing and sweating, I'd kind of forgotten about Annabelle until I heard her come in the door. "Mornin' Mr. O'Malley," she said as she approached.

I was hoping for more than that when she arrived, and she didn't disappoint me. Soon I felt her lips on my forehead. "Thank you," I said real clearly, I thought.

I knew it was clear when she kissed me again and said, "I owe you an extra kiss as a thank you for the TV set. My children were watching it this morning when I left for work."

"Good," I said, feeling like they just took Old Hickory's picture off the twenty dollar bill and replaced it with mine.

Then I heard her sigh, and she kind of whispered, "I hope no trouble comes from it. Lots of folks around here'll think I stole that old set of yours. They don't cotton to colored women getting gifts from white men."

I reached up and found her hand and gave it a gentle pat. "You. Friend!"

"I know, but maybe I shouldn't have taken it."

I was becoming more and more agitated, so to keep her from talking I snatched my hand back and used it along with the other to cover my ears. "Yours." I said with finality. "Yours."

That ended the discussion. To emphasis my feelings, I swatted at her butt as she began moving toward the other end of the room to retrieve my wheelchair. In my better days I would have given her behind a good one. This morning she just danced out of the way and laughed.

While she was wheeling me to breakfast, I saw a couple of shadows pass us. No one spoke to me, but that was nothing new. Normal people don't usually speak to people who can't see them or return their chatter. However, I thought it was strange no one said anything to Annabelle. They must have been visitors, because everyone talks to her.

A little farther down the hall, Annabelle leaned over and whispered in my ear. "I was afraid of that, Mr. O'Malley. When them two aides passed us by, Alice gave me the evil eye. I shouldn't have taken the TV. It's gonna be trouble. I just knows it."

Now, I do know from experience that sometimes people can make a good thing seem bad, and that's what that young white woman was doing, but I'll be damned if I was going to second guess my gesture, and I'll be double damned if I was going to let a damn young bitch take the joy out of my gift to Annabelle. "Stop!" I shouted.

My command was so clear, and Annabelle's reflexes so quick, if I hadn't been gripping the chair arm so tightly in my anger, my momentum would have sent me flying face first onto the floor when she stopped. Instead I stood up, and pointed back down the hall toward my room. Since I fully intended to confront Alice, I said, "Walk."

Finally catching on, Annabelle said, "Please don't, Mr. O'Malley. I don't want no more trouble. Let's go to breakfast."

Since I didn't have a plan of attack ready at that very moment, I did as she said and plopped back into the chair. The rest of the reason for capitulating was even more basic. I had smelled the toast, and it made me realize I was becoming hungrier by the second. Anyway, I live in a nursing home. I have all day to make things right.

Later that afternoon Alice came into my room to tidy it up. I was sitting on the bed, pretending to look out the window, and just hoping she'd open her big yap. She didn't fail me. "Some people around here are upset that you gave that darkie woman your TV set. Didn't you realize some of your own people might have wanted it, too?"

I turned and faced her. Then, I put on my best smile to let her know I understood and maybe even agreed with her. I've always believed that when people think you're stupid, they'll seek your level. Have you ever noticed how some adults talk to babies or animals? Anyway, when I had her ripe for my words, I let fly. "Alice, you act like shit." I don't know how clear it came out, because she was gone before I could catch my next breath, and I haven't seen her since.

Chapter 19

The Diary of a Sandhog

In early March of 1902, after a tear-filled parting with her parents, Florence and I left on the train for Boston. While I had traveled that way several times, the importance of this particular trip was not lost on me. No longer was I just another star-gazing youngster traveling alone to seek his fortune. Of the two of us, I was the seasoned veteran, in whose care Mr. and Mrs. Ferland had entrusted their family treasure, while Flo was the neophyte traveler approaching each new sight and exploring each new experience with wide-eyed innocence. In my heart I was sure the roles would blend over time as we became acclimated to our new circumstances, but for the moment she needed my hand to guide her.

Since my employment was scheduled to begin in a week's time, our task involved securing and furnishing a place to live in a safe neighborhood where Flo could make the transition from her parents' home in a tranquil Maine village into the unpredictable chaos of a metropolis. To this end, I decided to seek out Mrs. Borden for her advice. Secretly, I hoped she might agree to be more than a real estate consultant and for awhile serve as a surrogate mother to Flo until she was wise enough and confident enough to fend for herself in the big city.

After we arrived at South Station, I telephoned Mrs. Borden, and as I expected and hoped, she demanded I bring Florence to her for an immediate introduction followed by dinner. Rather than hire a taxi, I picked up our two suitcases, and with one in each hand, led my gawking wife down Tremont Street to catch the trolley.

Having learned a bit about my benefactor's desires from my previous one-year stay with her, I stopped at a florist shop along the way and purchased a half-dozen roses as a gift. Initially, Flo, who had never received such a gift, was surprised and miffed. However, by the time the streetcar had let us off near my old rooming house, I had convinced her of the wisdom of my actions, and she was fine with it.

When we reached Mrs. Borden's on Oxford Street, I put down the grips and rang the bell. In an instant the door opened and Mrs. Borden reached out to Flo and said, "Come in, dear! Come in!" and whisked her into the parlor. Meanwhile, I struggled with the bags and left them in the entry hall. By the time I entered the parlor, Flo had been given the seat of honor, Mrs. Borden's favorite antique blue velvet chair.

"You are even more beautiful than I imagined," she said as she busied herself with bringing the hassock for Flo's feet to make her more comfortable. "I'm making some tea, dear. Would you like some?"

Not waiting for a definite answer, she left the parlor for the kitchen. Of course, I knew the tea question was not asked of me because although I had entered the room, as yet Mrs. Borden hadn't acknowledged my presence.

While she was gone, I walked over to Flo and placed the roses across her lap. I then sarcastically bowed and groveled at her feet before backing away from her presence to the far side of the parlor. Studying her from that distance, the picture I saw in my mind was Cleopatra lounging on her barge. Still, Mrs. Borden was right about one thing. My wife was extremely beautiful.

In a short time our hostess returned carrying a tray with a teapot, small vessels of cream and sugar and four cups with saucers. She placed them on the coffee table and proceeded to pour a cup for Cleopatra. "Do you take cream or sugar, dear?" she asked.

When Flo shook her head to both, Mrs. Borden handed her the cup with a smile. In return, Flo handed her the roses. "These are for you," she said.

"I love roses, dear. Thank you so much." Then turning to me as if I'd just entered the room, she said, "I'm glad you're still on your feet, John. Would you mind marching down to Mrs. Florence Baker's home and fetching her. She's joining us for dinner."

Flo must have spotted my annoyance, because with my former landlady facing me, she grinned and bade me be off with a queenly wave of her hand.

To help hasten my journey, Mrs Borden said, "You do know Florence Baker lives in the corner house." While part of me was pleased by the lady of the house accepting my new wife, another part of me was irritated by her patronizing me. I knew as well as she did where Mrs. Baker lived. I'd been there many times.

Just for spite, I took my own sweet time putting on my jacket, but our hostess was so busy gushing over Flo, she took no notice. All I heard was, "Florence, dear, you are so thoughtful to bring me roses." Then I slammed the door behind me and trudged past the three houses to Mrs. Baker's home.

Along the way my mind conjured up a question. Why was I, who'd known Mrs. Borden well for almost a year, being dealt with as a servant, while a woman she'd just met was treated like royalty? The only answers that came to mind were maybe she hoped Flo would become the daughter she never had if even for a short time. Or, perhaps she missed her granddaughter and wanted another young woman to care about.

When Mrs. Baker opened the door, she immediately erased my pique with a warm embrace and a bright smile. "John, how nice of you to fetch me. I wanted a few moments alone with you to congratulate you on your wedding and share my best wishes."

On the walk back she asked me to carry the large, chocolate cake she'd baked in honor of the occasion "CAREFULLY IN BOTH HANDS" while she gently held onto my arm. At least she acknowledged my presence.

When Mrs. Borden greeted us, or rather Florence Baker, at the front door, she immediately grabbed her hand and said, "Come Florence, you have to meet our charming guest. She brought me roses." Then, noticing me still standing in the foyer waiting for instructions, she said, "Just place the cake on the counter in the kitchen, John, and join us."

Upon my return to the parlor, I witnessed an elaborate introduction of Flo to Florence Baker and an ensuing conversation filled with exclamations and praise. I sought refuge on the end of the couch within earshot of their chatter but out of the direct line of fire where I cocooned until dinner was announced. I was impressed. Women never seem to run out of things to talk about.

Despite my earlier reservations, dinner went exceedingly well. Mrs. Borden served a delicious lamb ragout over noodles, with carrots and a side of strawberry gelatin. Mrs. Baker's sumptuous cake was served for dessert. During the meal, the conversation centered on where Flo and I were going to live.

"I think they should settle right here in Brookline," Mrs. Borden said. "There are some lovely established apartments in the neighborhoods near the trolley. They would be near us, so we could make sure Florence is looked after during the day while John is on the job."

Mrs. Baker demurred. "That's a nice idea, Elizabeth, but those places are quite dear. You're forgetting that a new couple needs to purchase furniture and establish a household." She shrugged. "Anyway, what makes you think a young woman would choose to associate with a couple of old fuddy-duddies like us. She may want some gay company." She turned to Flo. "Isn't that right, dear?"

"Oh, Mrs. Baker, I would like to spend time with both of you. You are very kind, and I could learn so much from you."

Our hostess beamed. "See, Florence, she likes my idea."

Flo said, "It's a lovely idea, Mrs. Borden, but I will defer the decision of where we live to my husband and concur in his choice." She reached toward me, patted my hand and smiled.

Finally entering the discussion, I said, "Considering everything, I believe we'll look in Newton. It's near the streetcar, and since Newton is the nearest suburb to the west of Brookline, it wouldn't be far from you ladies. Also, because it has some newer, more modest dwellings whose rents are within our price range, it seems like a better choice."

"I think that's an excellent analysis, John."

"Thank you, Mrs. Baker. I think so, too, especially since we will most likely only live there a year."

"A year?" Mrs. Borden exclaimed. "Why only a year?"

"Because, after this job ends, we may be moving on to Baltimore. The work seems to be more plentiful there."

"All the more reason to search out Newton," Mrs. Baker said with finality. A few minutes passed with small talk and smiles before Mrs. Baker rose to her feet and said, "I've thoroughly enjoyed the evening, but I must take my leave. I have a morning appointment with my solicitor and need to get to bed."

I stood as well and said, "It's nearly nine, and we'll have to be going, too. Although I haven't made any arrangements, I did check with the desk at the Brighton Arms as we passed by on the way here, and they assured me they had a good deal of availability. Flo and I will walk you home on the way there, Mrs. Baker."

Mrs. Borden said, "You shall do no such thing, John. You will stay in your old room tonight and every other night until you are settled."

I quickly thanked her. My explicit reason for not making a reservation at the hotel had just been affirmed.

"Are you sure, Mrs. Borden?" Flo asked.

"As sure as I'm standing here, dear, and," she added, "as sure as I am that John will walk Florence home, and then on his return will carry the bags upstairs. She tossed me a look that left no opening for any modifications or refusal. "Meanwhile, you and I will examine the room and make sure it suits you."

That night Flo and I abstained from any newlywed behavior that might have awakened Mrs. Borden's slumber in the adjoining room.

The next morning I awoke before Flo, dressed quietly and tip-toed down to the kitchen. Mrs. Borden was baking bread. I poured myself a cup of tea from the pot on the stove, and chatted with her until she finished.

During the conversation she brought up Thomas' name in passing, and I realized my only communication from him since the wedding four months before had come in the form of a note telling me to report to work on March 16th. That was a long time to be without any newsy tidbits or to know what was happening in his life. Not that I was surprised. Boomer would never be judged a prolific letter writer. However, I had imagined my Best Man might have contacted me within that period to see how married life suited me. This was especially true since I'd written him each month with details. Or maybe that was my mistake, since knowing we were getting along well took away any excuse he had for writing back.

I asked Mrs. Borden, "Have you heard from Thomas?"

"Thomas is under a spell."

"A spell?"

"That vixen he met at your wedding, Prudence, I think her name is, has taken all the Irish out of him."

I laughed. "You mean he's quit drinking?"

She scowled. "He's quit the pub, he's lost his spirited ways, and he's stopped coming to dinner to see his aunt. He spends all his time with that woman."

"Prudence is a wonderful person, Mrs. Borden. It sounds like he's in love."

"If that were only so, I'd be pleased for him, but that is too out-of-character for me to accept." She lowered her voice. "The woman has him acting like a Congregationalist. That's no way for an Irish boy to be."

I tried to picture Boomer as a sober, soft-spoken sandhog, but the image wouldn't come into focus. Then, I recalled my earlier conversation with him about his Thomas-Boomer split personality. "Maybe your nephew has shed his Boomer skin and become the person for whom his name was intended."

With a sigh of resignation she said, "May that be the case, then."

Before sitting down to eat my oatmeal and toast, I walked up behind her and placed a firm hand on each shoulder. "Either way, I'll still call him my best friend."

She smiled and said, "You are a good boy, John."

While I ate, I considered plans to share Boomer and Prudy's company before I started work the following week. Assuming they would even consider coming all the way to Newton to see us, Flo and I had to find an apartment to live in and furnish. Considering the monumental details involved, I quickly realized the task was far too daunting to promote. Seeing Boomer on the first day of work would have to do.

After I finished breakfast and washed and dried my dishes at the sink, I started toward the stairs with the idea of waking Flo so we could start our day together. Before I left the room my hostess hailed me. With extreme sadness in her voice and manner, she pleaded, "John, please don't abandon my nephew."

"I'd never do that," I vowed.

For the next two days, Flo and I looked at rentals before picking out a one-bedroom second-floor apartment in a three-decker on the east edge of Newton. True to my word, I made sure the building was near enough to the older ladies for Flo to walk to their homes. It was also near the trolley and appropriate both in size and expense to fit us perfectly. On the third day since arriving in Boston, we made our first furniture purchase, a double bed we found in Quincy Market. The merchant trucked it to our new home, and that night, after thanking Mrs. Borden for our stay, we walked hand-in-hand under a moonlit sky to share the joy of our new bed in our otherwise bare apartment.

The following morning Flo made tea in an old pot Mrs. Baker had given us. Since I was the only one fully dressed, I skipped down the flight of stairs and trotted off to the baker's shop to buy two sticky buns and a loaf of rye bread. Next, I popped into the butcher's a few doors down, had him slice some ham and picked up a quart of milk and a pound of butter at the grocer's. The whole trip took less than thirty minutes and covered a total of four blocks.

Once I'd climbed the stairs to the apartment, Flo, now dressed for the day, served the tea and we ate the sticky buns and polished off some rye bread with butter. Then, Flo made ham sandwiches for lunch which we packed into the bakery bag and carried with us to eat on the street as we spent the better part of the day exploring the neighborhood and the various stores. By the time we returned home, we'd purchased some kitchen utensils and items like flour, lard, condiments and other items so Flo could begin cooking for the two of us. We also purchased two used wooden chairs and a small maple table which, when delivered, would work well for our meals and those times we might be reading or conversing or otherwise not in our bed. For the rest of the week, we kept so busy we never even thought of entertaining Boomer and Prudy.

My first contact with him came on the job. We were working ten feet down and had just filled several barrow loads of debris which I had dispatched to a large pile in an empty spot on the surface between our hole and another one forty feet away. When I returned, the men in our crew were taking a cigarette break, all except Boomer. I never did smoke, and Boomer never did either in the hole, although he was known to light up at the pub with a stout in his hand and a few more in his belly. I asked a test question based on the information volunteered by his aunt. "Have you quit smoking?"

The answer was decidedly Boomeresque. "Fags aren't good for ye, John. It's bad enough I got a job that can put an end to ye," he snapped his fingers, "just like that. I don't need to be huffin' and puffin' on my way to the devil's workshop."

"So, have you quit?"

"Aye, now that I got me a girl I want to please for a long, long time."

I decided to play dumb knowing he was referring to Prudy. "Do you mean your girl back in Ireland?"

He acted shocked. "Married life got your brain addled, John? I'm talkin' about Prudence Harkness from your own wedding."

"Oh," I said. "I thought that was a one-nighter, nothing more."

His face turned crimson, and I could see his anger building. "Don't even think my Prudy would do such a thing with the likes of me or any man. We're gettin' married."

"Good for you. You'll make a great couple." Then, I defended myself. "But, Boom, you'll have to agree there have been a few nights when you've wandered home with a lass you never saw again."

"None I ever remembered later," he laughed.

"Because you were drunk."

He laughed. "Aye, maybe that's why I'm not rememberin' 'em."

"So, when are you getting married?"

"When we get a few things worked out."

I began laughing and said, "Like going to the pubs?"

"Nay. That's no problem. I just don't go no more for now. Come fall will be soon enough after we're married."

"Don't tell me you're staying sober to trick her into marrying you and then you're going to start drinking again?"

"You got it all wrong, John. I'm a man of principle, I am."

I shook my head in wonder. "Then, explain yourself."

"That I will. It's this way. There's three things Prudy's got against me. Me drinking, me swearing and me bein' so loud. Other than that she'll marry me in a damn Galway minute."

"But, you don't intend to change any of those things?"

He put his arm around my shoulder and said, "Hear me out, friend. Prudy has three things I don't like about her, too. She's a damn suffragist, she's in the Temperance Union and worst of all, she's a Congregationalist. Since we've been in love, she's sworn off all three of them vices."

"But those aren't vices."

"They are to me, just as drinking, swearing and talking loud are to her," he said. "So, I figure it this way. We'll both hold out until we're married to prove our love for each other." He dropped his arm from my shoulder and grinned. "Now, John, since I don't expect Prudy will swear off her vices forever, when the devil leads her by the hand back to her first vice, I'll be goin' back to drinkin' at the pub. The second one, I'll swear again and the third one, I'll be as loud as I ever was." He clapped his hands. "So you see the whole marriage thing is a give and take."

"What if she stays true to her word?"

He grinned, "Then, I'll have to let her know I don't give a shite if she votes or not and hope she becomes a suffragist again so I can have a wee nip now and then."

I patted him on the back. "You've got it all figured out, haven't you, my friend?"

He nodded.

"Well, I'll have to give you credit for that."

"And, I won't ever smoke again."

"Why is that?" I asked tentatively.

"Because I don't like it that much."

While we were walking back to the others who were awaiting Boomer's instructions, I suggested he go visit his aunt and tell her about his plans with Prudy. "She's not sure what you're up to, and she's lonely for her Thomas."

"Aye, you're a good boy for remindin' me, John. It would be a good time to visit me auntie while Thomas is in control of Boomer."

Throughout the summer and into autumn, I dug the caissons for the Mother House of the Christian Science Church and helped Mrs. Borden accept Prudy by convincing her that underneath his new veneer, Thomas was indeed still all Irish. That fall, both Flo and I stood up for Prudy and Boomer at their wedding. In addition, our son, Mike, was conceived in Boston, escaped from the womb in Kittery Point the following November sixth and grew up in Baltimore.

Chapter 20

MIKE O'MALLEY

I've often wondered why my parents always said I was raised in Baltimore. I can't quibble with their saying I was conceived in Boston because the gestation period fit comfortably into the period leading up to my birth in 1907. I also know I was born in Kittery Point because it says so on my birth certificate. But, the part about growing up in Baltimore was a bit of a stretch. It's true my mother brought me to Baltimore from Kittery Point to reunite with my father when I was eighteen months old in March of 1909, and we didn't permanently move away from Baltimore until September of 1924, after my seventeenth birthday. Still, the time line doesn't tell the whole story. I know because during that time we lived in six different apartments, three of which were in New York City matching the three we inhabited in Baltimore.

In addition, I changed schools and neighborhood friends every other year for the last twelve of those years. An embarrassing sidebar to two of these upheavals led to my being deemed so slow in my educational development that I was forced to repeat the third and fifth grades. Since there were no standardized tests or even an oral interview at the time to determine my ability to proceed to the next level, my placement depended entirely on the whim of my next teacher after a cursory look at my transcript. In both cases, I was considered too dull to move on.

There have been times in the past when I've cursed the misfortune of having a job-chasing father that kept me hopscotching from grade to grade. While normal kids lumbered through school one grade at a time, I was either frenetically trying to catch up or hopelessly bored with my class work. Unlike a traditional student, I never had the luxury of occasionally treading water during my academic whirlpool. Moreover, the lucky non-movers had a constant supply of old friends and acquaintances to enjoy, while I was forever foraging for new relationships. Even when I was planted long enough to grow a friendship, it seldom had time to flower before we were on the move again.

In 1918 when I was eleven, I'd just enrolled in a new school and learned I was about to repeat the fifth grade. That night when my father came home from work, I confronted him. While I've long ago forgiven him for adding to my stressful adolescent years, on that occasion I was morbidly upset with his incessant moving. After listening patiently to my rant, he placed a big arm around my shoulder and quietly and almost apologetically explained that moving from job to job was an integral part of being a sandhog. "Once a foundation is dug, a tunnel bored or the work in a caisson completed, I have to move on, or not work at all. I know all this moving is hard on you and your mother, but, son, I also have a responsibility to make sure you have a nice place to live and good food to eat." He reached over and patted my stomach. "Your mother is keeping that tinder box full isn't she, Mike?"

"Yeah," I answered, but I was upset that he wasn't taking my concern seriously enough. I pulled away and stated emphatically, "I won't repeat fifth grade. I'm already older than all the other kids."

He scrunched up his face and slowly shook his head. "That is a real problem, Mike, but I'm afraid I can't do a thing about it. You have to go to school." He was silent for a few moments until his concerned look faded and a grin crept onto his face. He squatted and placed his hands on his knees so our eyes were on the same level and said tentatively, "You know, Mike, we'll probably move again by next year."

"I suppose," I groaned.

"So, maybe next year you'll skip sixth grade altogether."

It didn't appease me at the time, but when I later returned to Washington Grade School in Baltimore, his prophecy came true. Not surprisingly, the decision to pass me on was made solely by the ectomorphic, spinster principal who stated clearly that my acceleration had nothing to do with my academic achievements and everything to do with my being too old and too big to be in the sixth grade.

As a direct result of my marred childhood, I swore I'd never put my own son, Tim, through the same regimen. I stuck with my resolve, too, because other than the first four years of his life when the Depression forced me to move from one sales position to another in different cities, he was able to spend his entire youth moving smoothly through the Rockford school system. He also had a wide ranging group of friends of both sexes whom he knew from school, church and his various sports activities. Even now, when I review the decision Sara and I made to stay in one place for Tim's sake, I feel an overwhelming pride that I'm sure Sara would also share with me if only her brain could comprehend it.

Looking back, I'm amazed at how well I coped with all the moving from apartment to apartment and school to school, starting over with new teachers and finding new friends. Sadly, nothing is earned in life without paying a price, and the price I paid turned out to be dear for me and my family. Early on, I learned to cope with all the pressures by fundamentally shutting down my emotions. In fact, I learned the skills so well that today I'm just no good with "feelings." Sadly, at the very time I could and should be of help to Tim, I'm totally useless. Even worse is the realization that the plan Sara and I concocted to protect Tim from some of the adversity I had to face in my childhood, may have led him to his difficulty coping with little Marie's death.

The one bright spot in his recovery seems to be transcribing the stories my father loves telling the cassette recorder. I'm not sure the finished product will be much of a read, but the process brings them together and helps dad's speech. Plus, dad sure loves to share his past. Since I'm an O'Malley, I have a flair for story-telling, too. That's why I decided to horn in on their project and tell some stories of my own. I'm hoping it's one way I might be comfortable letting some of my feelings see the light of day. Then, as Tim transcribes them, he'll see my love and concern for him as he works through his grief, and maybe we'll both feel better.

Today, I made another move. After chatting with my dad for a good twenty minutes, I grabbed the microphone off the table and started talking. He was so curious about what I was up to, he wheeled near me so as not to miss anything. Minutes later when he understood, his face lit up in the same huge smile I assume he usually reserves for Annabelle.

"I know you're having a really tough time, Tim. I wonder what Pete Grey would do? Do you remember him?

"In 1945, right after World War II, your mother and I decided to spend one of my two vacation weeks in St. Louis with her parents. By this time you were playing baseball and rooting for the Chicago Cubs to win the World Series. Until then, you'd never even seen a major league game. With the help of your grandfather, I procured tickets to several St. Louis Browns games. Both the American League Browns and the National League Cardinals shared Sportsmans Park at the time. What a kick it was for you and me to take the rickety, Cass Avenue street car down St. Louis Avenue to Vanderventer, walk the two blocks past the Carter Carburetor Company plant and enter Sportsmans Park. Each time we arrived early so you could take snapshots with your Brownie camera of any player who was willing to pose for you. We also watched them warm up and take batting practice. Since Phil Caveretta, the star first baseman with the Cubs, didn't play in any of these American League games, you latched onto Pete Grey of the Browns as your next favorite player, probably because he was a willing poser, kid-friendly and only had one arm.

"While I was impressed by Pete Grey's ability to successfully swing a bat and make contact with one arm, it was his outfield play that fascinated me. He'd catch the ball in the glove on his left hand, quickly stuff the glove and ball under the stump where his right arm had been, extract the ball and throw it on the run. It was quite a spectacle.

"Fortunately, because of your instant love for the player, Pete Grey became an inspiration. After that, whenever you became depressed by some failure or showed signs of giving up when you faced some obstacle, I'd remind you of all Pete Grey had overcome to play major league baseball with just one arm. All I had to say in those instances was, 'Tim, do you suppose Pete Grey would give up if he struck out in a crucial situation in a game?' Or, 'Wouldn't Pete Grey keep trying even if he got a C in math class?' It always worked and got you back on track."

Then, I added a message to the tape for Tim's benefit. "I hope remembering Pete Grey might still work its magic. I know it sounds corny, but what's the harm in trying. I love you and really want to help."

As I was leaving Dad's place, I began having second thoughts about my taped message to my son. However, by the time I was in the car and ready to drive away, I just knew Tim was going to take it the right way.

Chapter 21

MIKE O'MALLEY

I was in high school when I first became aware of the respect others had for the way my father, John O'Malley, did his job. Prior to that I had always thought he was just a manual laborer digging away in an outsized hole. Despite everyone else calling him Boomer, my parents insisted I use Uncle Thomas whenever I referred to their friend. It was he who set me straight during a brief history lesson while we were all playing cards at his and Aunt Prudy's apartment. Between deals, he explained how it was that my father was promoted to supervisor and became his boss, instead of the other way around. I could tell by the look on his face, my father was as interested in Boomer's explanation as I was.

Without any display of rancor, Uncle Thomas stated, "Me and a lot of the boys knew a lot more about sandhoggin' than your Da." He glanced at my father for a reaction. Seeing none, he continued. "But, he wasn't Irish, so he could get a lot more work out of the Negroes than any Irishman could." He flashed a wicked grin and said, "I hate to admit it, Mike, but John O'Malley is such a straight-up guy, he also gets more work out of them Irish boys than I ever could."

Uncle Thomas went on to explain how the Irish hold on the sandhog culture had changed rapidly during that time in the large eastern cities. "You see, Mike, when the first Irishmen came to America after the Potato Famine in the eighteen-fifties, they got stuffed into the tough jobs no other immigrant or native wanted. Before long so many of us became sandhogs, and we were so close-knit we controlled the underground jobs. He grinned at my father. "Without no Scotsman to bother us, we worked together, drank together and only trusted each other. Because we also got hurt together and died together, the boys also tended to marry colleens from the same families. These women knew the risks and accepted them." He pointed to his chest. "I'm the odd ball. Prudence is a Congregationalist, you know."

Thinking the women might be ready to give him some static, he peeked around to see who else might be listening. When he realized my dad and I comprised his total audience, he seemed a little deflated, but he restarted his monologue. I was glad he started up again. Being privy to man-talk, and especially the unedited monologues that escaped my charismatic Uncle Thomas' lips was always a highlight for a loosely rooted sixteen-year-old.

"The problem, Mike, is for the last ten years or so there's been so much new construction going on, the rich owners started hiring farm Negroes from Virginia to do our work. They say they're doin' it because there aren't enough Irishmen to get all the work done, but the boys all know they hire the black men because they work for peanuts. Whole freight trains full of 'em come into Baltimore and the other big cities every week. They want to learn our trade so they can steal our jobs. Hell, in New York City, black men from the islands who can't even speak English are takin' our jobs because they work for practically nothin'.

"It probably ain't right," he said, "but there are times when a black guy gets injured on the job, and the Irish boys cheer as he's being carried to the surface on a stretcher by his own kind. Then, too, if we ever so much as touch one of the Negroes, we have to stay alert or some of the black bastards will try to get even. It's pretty damn tense down in the hole during these times."

My father finally entered the conversation. "By the end of the Great War, the bitterness had reached a point to where management had to face up to a huge dilemma. While there were still a few elite Irish crews who took on the toughest jobs, there weren't enough of them. However, when they tried all-Negro units, they didn't work out. Lots of brawn, but no leadership. They were like a team of horses with no driver. Every job took longer." My father gestured to Uncle Thomas. "So, as Boomer already said about the integrated crews, the morale was awful, the accident rate soared and all the daily turmoil caused so many construction delays company profits plummeted.

"That's when they promoted me," my father said. "Apparently, they thought it was more important to have a supervisor who could get along well enough with both groups, even if he didn't have as much construction experience as a guy like Uncle Thomas. So they put me in charge of an integrated group of the best men from each camp." He looked down at the floor and chose his words carefully. Nodding in Boomer's direction, he said, "The truth is, Boomer and the other foremen knew more about caisson work than I did, so I left everyone alone and only intervened to keep the two factions from killing one another."

Just the way he said it, I detected something in his tone that made me question him. "Would they really try to kill each other?"

"Yeah, they would, I'm sorry to say. They tried to get me, too. I guess that's why guys always point toward the ground when they describe hell. Life underground is just like that–pure hell. But, once my Negro workers realized I wasn't Irish, either by birth, habits,"...he used his hand to pantomime taking a drink... "or bias, they always did what I asked of them and more. Similarly, when the Irish workers determined from my words and actions that I wasn't a Negro apologist, they also came around. With Boomer as foreman of one crew, and Otis Lundy, the other, the fighting stopped, and we moved a lot of rock and subsoil."

I noticed the grin on Boomer's face as he said, "Also, Mike, it didn't hurt that because your Da was built like a brick outhouse, if anyone tried to mess with his hogs, he would and could whip them with a quick knock-out punch to the gut or head."

Boomer really puffed me up when he said, "Mike, your Da is the best boss I ever had, including me. He makes friends with the Irish boys and the Negroes, because he keeps his word and treats everyone fair."

Then, my father laughed out loud and said, "Boomer knows that if he'd been supervising these guys, they'd still be killing each other just for fun."

The entire conversation gave me a whole new perspective. From that day forward I had a far greater respect for what my father went through to see that my mother and I had a good life.

Chapter 22

The Diary of a Sandhog

Each time we returned to Baltimore for another brief stay, Flo and I found a larger or fancier apartment within the original city limits, or as it was called, the "inside property." The current stop was on Redwood Street, which prior to the end of the Great War had been named German Street. While the neighborhood make-up stayed primarily German-American, most of the residents favored a street name change that would appease the majority of Americans who were prone to blame Germans for the Kaiser's War which had been raging for more than a year.

Flo liked to call the German women Scrubby Dutch because of their penchant for getting down on their hands and knees and scrubbing the outside steps and sidewalks around their homes. In fact, they were squeaky clean in virtually everything they did. Spit in the street in their presence and you risked an all-female altercation that might, if conditions were right, include some fly-ing pots and pans. Such was their fanaticism for cleanliness.

While some saw this German passion against filth as a humor-ous obsession, those who were staunch believers in germ theory commended their scrubbing for holding the line on the worst of the current communicable diseases like cholera and tuberculo-sis. Actually, by the time we arrived in Baltimore, the former had been eradicated by the more efficient handling of the city's sew-age. However, consumption raged. Thousands of people, mostly from the poor and lower classes were infected, and the tidy, more affluent Germans scrubbed and scrubbed to keep it out of their neighborhoods.

However, in 1917, when Mike was ten, a new killer arrived on the scene. Suddenly, people of all ages, and especially young children like our son, were sick and dying from influenza. In our area of town, this new threat intensified our neighbors' efforts to rid their world of the killer. Despite this, in the period of a week, three of Mike's playmates were stricken, and one, Peter Schmidt, died. That was enough to convince Flo and I that Baltimore was no place for our only son to be living. The next day, we put him on the train to Portsmouth, hoping he could avoid exposure to the disease by essentially being "quarantined" for the summer in Kittery Point. Our decision turned out to be a good one. Instead of shutting him up in our apartment to avoid getting sick, he made new friends, fished in both the tidewaters and the ocean with his Grandpa Ferland and generally basked in the loving care of his grandparents. Besides fishing for the whole summer, my father-in-law also drove Mike to Portsmouth in his new Model T Ford several times a week so he could play baseball in the fresh air with some older youngsters. That was his first real encounter with baseball, and as the summer wore on, he developed a love for the game and skills far beyond his years.

In late August, Mike returned to our apartment in Baltimore and reunited with his mother and me. A few weeks later, he entered still another grade school and repeated the third grade.

Although I seldom talked with Mike back then about my current work projects, I discussed each specific job in detail with Flo. During our stays in Baltimore, I supervised crews who were still rebuilding the city long after the horrendous fire of 1904. I excavated the B&O Building, another twenty story structure that housed the gas and electric company and worked for two years on a major sewer project. I also supervised the underground work on an expansion of the Maryland Steel Company. During this same period, with Boomer at my side, I was the caisson supervisor for several new skyscrapers in New York City.

In 1923 following our move from New York back to Baltimore, Flo and I were saddened by the sudden passing of Mrs. Borden. While her death shook us, Boomer took it especially hard. As a consequence and because we always worked together, Boomer and Prudy became constant visitors to whatever apartment we were living in at the time. Since Prudy was the only constant in Flo's life, and Boomer in mine, it was only natural that most of our family's social life involved the two of them. In addition, since they had yet to have any children of their own, Mike was allowed to sample our adult conversation and suck up all the adoration that naturally flowed toward an only child.

As I recall, virtually all of our Saturday evenings were spent either at our apartment or theirs, eating and playing cards. When we went to their house, Prudy prepared delicious meals, but as a rule her menus were not as elaborate as my wife's. Meatloaf with candied apples or fresh tongue with horseradish were especially good, but not as fine as Flo's presentations.

Flo was a fabulous cook. She was also adventuresome. One week she might present an entree of roasted leg of lamb, the next beefsteak and then for a special occasion, she might prepare a pheasant. In my mind, each meal would be the envy of any chief of state. I was sure one of the stout ex-Presidents of my childhood, namely Taft, might have eaten as much as us, but I'm sure he never ate as well.

Chapter 23

MIKE O'MALLEY

The highlight of most family evenings for me, besides the meals, was playing cribbage with Uncle Thomas. We played for pennies. For some reason, Uncle Thomas always held bad cards, or so he said when I beat him, which was most of the time. While I played a decent game of cribbage, his run of bad luck tested the outer limits of the Laws of Probability. I'd catch him winking at my father after suffering another loss and reaching into his pocket to pay up. "Your son is too good for me, John," he'd say. Then he'd quickly pick up the cards, declare, "Suckers deal" and begin dealing out the cards for the next game which he'd also usually manage to lose.

When I was eleven and twelve, I never questioned why I consistently lost to my father and mother, but always beat Uncle Thomas. Apparently, the ever-growing stream of Uncle Thomas' pennies that found their way into my bank had clouded my thinking. However, by the time I was a wise-to-the-ways-of-the-world fifteen, I began to suspect there was something fishy about our cribbage games. My first clue came when I caught Uncle Thomas breaking up his hand by tossing his best cards into the crib. After I saw this happen several times, I realized no one but a terrible cribbage player or a fool would make such mistakes. Since Uncle Thomas was neither, it finally occurred to me that he might be throwing the games so I could win.

One night as I lay in bed listening to the adult conversations through the paper thin wall between my bedroom and the living room, I heard my father bawl out Uncle Thomas. "Boomer, no one wins all the time. The boy needs to learn how to lose, so you've got to play him straight."

I've heard my mother say many times, "The truth hurts," and yet, until that moment, I never knew what she meant. However, what Uncle Thomas intended as a generous gesture, had robbed me of my first real taste of success in the card-playing adult world. I thought I was a winner. Finding out I'd been duped made me feel betrayed. Since I loved Uncle Thomas, I spent the time between visits trying to figure out a way to make him understand my disappointment without making him feel bad about it.

The next Saturday evening while the women fussed over dinner in the kitchen, I said casually, "Do you want to play cribbage, Uncle Thomas?"

I watched him glance at my father and then say, "I suppose." While my father set up the card table in the living room, I went back to my bedroom and brought back a small bag of thirty pennies that I'd previously fished out of the slit in my bank one by one. Once we were seated across from each other and before he dealt the cards, I counted out fifteen pennies and pushed them over in front of him. He eyed me and glanced at my father, who shrugged. After dropping a couple of cards while he was shuffling, Uncle Thomas finally began to deal. Before picking up his hand, he asked, "What's the money for, Mike?"

I'd been practicing my speech and was ready for him. "We've been playing with your pennies all this time. Now that I'm fifteen, I want to see if I'm good enough to play with mine."

Uncle Thomas turned to my father. "This smells like your idea, John O'Malley."

My dad shook his head. "I think you're wrong, Boomer. You'd better play your best, because it seems the boy wants to beat your butt."

He sighed. "Aye, so he does."

We played four games, and I lost them all. While I was proud of the way I handled the situation, I sure didn't like losing twelve pennies. Later that evening when I was in the bathroom peeing, Uncle Thomas walked in on me. "Oh, I'm sorry, lad. I didn't know you were in here." However, before backing out, he placed a shiny, silver Walking Liberty half-dollar on the edge of the sink. I looked at it and at him. He said nothing, but his eyes sent a message that this transaction was just between the two of us. I mouthed a 'thank you' and dribbled pee on my shoe.

Chapter 24

MIKE O'MALLEY

I also heard a lot of talk about drinking alcohol during these get-togethers, but I never actually saw anyone take a drink. Both homes were led by matriarchs who were staunch members of the Women's Christian Temperance Union, or WCTU. Many of their waking hours were spent railing against the perils of Demon Rum. Unbeknownst to me at the time, Uncle Thomas apparently drank more than his share before going dry to marry Aunt Prudence. The sudden and continued change in habits baffled his Irish cronies and caused my father, who probably never drank alcohol anyway, to tease him unmercifully.

"Boom, you swore you were going to start drinking again once you were married. That's been five years ago. Where's your honor? Don't you keep your word?"

"You don't know nothin,' John O'Malley," he deadpanned. "Anyway, it ain't been no five years. I been hitched for six...long... dry...years." Chuckling, he began counting on his fingers. "Aye, it's been more like six years, three months and eleven days since I had me last stout, but who's countin'? Truly, John, it really don't mean nothin' to me now."

"I can see that," my dad said, laughing. "Still, you're a good man, Boom. I admire you for it."

"Most good Irishmen think I'm weak for quittin.' Only a Scotsman would see some good in it." He turned to me. "You listen to your Da, Mike. He don't bellow about the evils of drink like your Ma, Prudy and the other ladies from the WCTU, but he lives what he says. Your Da ain't no hypocrite."

He was right. Throughout my adolescent years, I listened to my mother berate those poor souls who succumbed to liquor's siren call, while my father was silent on the subject, and to my knowledge, dry. My own version of Prohibition ended when I went off to college and was out from behind my mother's skirts. My first drink, drunken episode and mild hangover occurred on the first night and second morning after my arrival at the Missouri School of Mines in Rolla, Missouri. It was more than introductory. Two nights later, I surpassed the intensity of the first experience by indulging so heavily I couldn't make my morning classes because my head was in the toilet, and I had a splitting headache.

Looking back, it's safe to say booze has played a big role in my life. To say I was, or am a problem drinker, would depend on who was saying it. No boss of mine or my wife, Sara, ever suggested I give it up. Although alcohol was ever-present in my adult life, their silence confirmed my own thoughts. If drinking didn't interfere with what was important to me and my family, why worry about it?

Lately, when I face the truth, I realize there have been times over the years when maybe I should have given my drinking a second thought. Like now with Sara going rapidly downhill. Since for me, drinking does act as a shock absorber, one would think it would make my life better. However, it doesn't. It only complicates things. For example, I think my showing up at my son, Tim's, house loaded one evening may have had something to do with his and Claire's coolness toward me. Whether I'm imagining this or not isn't easily determined. I do know that since Marie died it has strained our relationship. Moreover, I do know for sure my grandson, Michael, avoids me. I would, too, if I thought my grandfather was an alcoholic.

The last time I was invited to their home, I deliberately didn't drink a thing before I arrived, and Tim still shunted Michael off to his room right after dinner under the guise of doing his homework. That hurt. Especially when I heard the TV blaring from his room.

Since then I hardly ever see Claire, and I only see Tim if I chase him down at work or run into him at my father's. I realize they've lost a daughter, but for all practical purposes, I've lost a wife. Wouldn't that be a clue for a son to invite his father into his life once in awhile? Sometimes, when I face reality, I realize I don't add much to our relationship anyway. But, unlike my ever-sober, rock-solid father who's always been in charge of his habits, I know what I'm doing to myself, and why I'm doing it. I take full responsibility for being irresponsible. I'm sixty-six years old and stubborn, too, just like my father. No matter how much misery I cause myself and others, I don't intend to change, although my gut tells me I should go see the old man more often than I do.

One time before WWII when my wife, Sara, and I were in our early thirties and Tim was a toddler, my mother came to visit us in Chicago. Just as Sara was putting the finishing touches on the meal she hoped would impress her mother-in-law, I, without thinking, casually mixed a pitcher of martinis. As was our custom when we were alone, a martini or two before and with dinner made the pressures of the day disappear and the dinner hour more meaningful. Of course, that was when we were alone.

I can still see the pained expression on my mother's face as she stood over me while I was stirring. Since I was well into the process and couldn't disguise in any way the intended use of the finished product, I just kept mixing and bracing myself for the scathing condemnation I knew was coming. Instead, she remained silent. I was baffled. In many ways, her silence was more disconcerting than a maternal fit of anger.

When I couldn't pretend that continuing to stir would somehow make the cocktail any tastier, I said, using my finest gallows humor, "So, Mom, shall I pour one for you?"

Already ducking in case she launched a physical assault, I received the shock of my life. "Just a taste, please," she replied, "to give the devil in me a treat."

"But, Mom..."

"If my son and daughter-in-law aren't afflicted because of it, I guess it's all right for an old lady to see what all the fuss is about." She took a sip and then another and then smiled meekly. "And, Mike, don't you ever tell your father about this, or I'll skin you alive."

Sometime later, my father informed me that upon her return to East St. Louis where they lived at the time, my mother gave him an earful about Sara and I drinking martinis. "I hope you'll keep your drinking under wraps the next time she visits," he said. "You know how she is about liquor."

That was the first time in my life I realized my dear mother was a bit of a hypocrite. It wouldn't be the last, but it was comforting to see her climb down from her pedestal from time to time when my dad wasn't looking.

Chapter 25

TIM O'MALLEY

In 1952 when I was sixteen, I was seated on the porch steps with my head resting in my hands and my elbows on my knees on a hot, sticky Saturday night in August. Around ten-thirty, a passing car suddenly screeched to a stop, backed up and parked facing the wrong way at the curb under our corner streetlight. "Hey, Tim. Come here. I want you to see what I've done to this baby." The voice and vehicle belonged to my friend, Gibby, who preferred yelling to talking in a normal tone of voice.

He began using a flashlight's beam and the loud patter of a circus barker to point out the features of his unique vehicle. "Overhead cam, four on the floor. Man, this bear can really roar!"

I was impressed, but at that hour, I would have been content with a quiet visual inspection. However, that never would have met Gibby's need to extol the car's virtues to a larger audience. Happily for Gibby, the crowd grew by two. The gregarious black Lab who typically aired his drunken master, Mr. Keegan, late at night, decided he needed some sober companionship and pulled the helpless man to us in a series of lurches. To announce his own presence, the dog lifted his leg to anoint a tire and flopped down in the grass to listen to Gibby's commentary. Mr. Keegan joined him on the ground, except unlike his companion, he promptly fell asleep with his back against the trunk of a maple.

A second man appeared on the scene, my father, Mike O'Malley. Now, Dad was an amiable sort who enjoyed companionship at any hour of the day or night, particularly if he'd filled his glass a few times during the evening. Also, it was his habit during torrid weather to sleep downstairs on the couch in front of the fan in just his Jockey shorts. Apparently, Gibby's yammering had awakened him and curiosity brought him to view the curbside festivities. Always a modest guy, Dad must have realized he couldn't appear in public so scantily clad, so he slipped into the dining room, yanked off the lace tablecloth which now barely covered his modesty, joined the group and embarrassed the heck out of me.

The centerpiece of the presentation that followed was a dark blue '47 Chevy that had been purchased from a salvage yard for $22.50. The owner/presenter, real name George Gibson, my friend since grade school, began telling his audience, "The car had been in so many accidents the insurance company totaled it." I guessed, from their point of view, the car couldn't be restored to its former glory without expending far more cash than the heap of broken metal was worth.

Of course, they hadn't viewed the wreck through Gibby's enthusiastic eyes. Nor were they used to someone possessing his patient creativity when it came to fixing all things mechanical. Although his academic achievements could be counted on one finger, the expressive middle one of his right hand, which on many occasions had incited the wrath of his teachers during his extended high school stay, he was a genius with tools. In the case of this vehicle, that meant a wrench, crowbar, welding torch and metal saw.

The singular sedan we viewed that night was not, nor ever would be, one of those roaring chick-attracting hotrods that some of our peers raced around town. Nonetheless, because I admired the effort that Gibby had expended to rejuvenate the car to its present condition, it held a certain charm for me. Also, knowing he'd spent the bulk of his time under the hood rebuilding the motor kept me from being shocked by the vehicle's outward appearance. For example, the doors. There weren't any. They had been so damaged by the original owner that Gibby, rather than replacing them, just tore them off and sold them for scrap. The second deviation from the norm was the quilt that covered the front seats. Having slept over many times at his parents' house during junior high, I recognized the covering as the one that had previously adorned my bed in their spare bedroom. The third was the one-of-a-kind back seat. Instead of fixing the stained and torn upholstery, he'd ripped out the cushions and the frame that held them and filled the void with two old single bed mattresses, one on top of the other. When my dad raised an eyebrow and queried him about the functionality of the configuration, Gibby became uncharacteristically inarticulate and began stuttering, "Sometimes...I...ah...carry...ah passengers back there."

Later that night, after Fido had escorted Mr. Keegan home, and Dad had seen fit to return to his fan, I told Gibby, "I really think your vehicle is slick."

He beamed at my compliment. "It's a dream ready to happen," he said cryptically. "I'll let you drive it some time."

Since I was only sixteen-and-a-half, one year younger than Gibby, and light years less worldly, I reacted to his offer as if he'd promised me a million bucks. After all, I'd been licensed for a mere six months, and was only a summer removed from learning the rudiments of driving in my Grandpa O'Malley's circular drive in Michigan. I considered his offer in the same vain as if The New York Central had asked me to be the engineer on the Twentieth Century Limited from Chicago to New York. "Wow! That would be great!"

Two months later in early October I took him up on his offer when Henrietta Herdklotz, who I was to find out later had conjoined with most of the male members of the senior class, set her sights on me solely because I appeared virginal and was trending toward stardom on the basketball court. Since she was a good-looking chick, I was flattered and a bit awed when she stopped me in the school hallway and said, "Would you go with little ol' me to the Sadie Hawkins Dance a week from Saturday?"

"Sure," I said, looking down at the floor, too dazzled to look her in the eye or elsewhere. After all, as Gibby observed, she was something to watch both coming and going. When she approached, she had those fashionably pointed knockers that could puncture a lung if she got too close. Going away, her bottom swung from side to side like two volley balls in a gunny sack. What guy wouldn't say yes?

While I'd be the first to admit I didn't know a whole lot about dating, I sensed a looming problem. Until then, I hadn't been entrusted with the family car. While I deemed it acceptable to be driven by a parent to my little-boy dates, the movies or a house party where we played spin-the-bottle, I could only imagine Henrietta Herdklotz's reaction if I showed up at her house with my father playing chauffeur. Immature as I was, I still understood that our upcoming date was my entree into manhood, and any deviation from the norm, like not having wheels, might set back my development for years to come. That's why, with the dance rapidly approaching, I bypassed begging for the family car and decided on a different approach–lying. I told my parents I was double-dating with Gibby.

The next day during lunch hour, I told Gibby, "I have a date with Henrietta Herdklotz."

"Really!" he said, his expression full of shock.

"She asked me to the Sadie Hawkins Dance." Then I pleaded, "Can I use your Dream Machine?"

Before I could go through the rest of the spiel I'd been perfecting all morning to guarantee his agreement, he flashed a huge grin and said, "You can use it. Just don't forget your rubbers."

"I won't, Gibby," but it wasn't until after the dance when I was following Henrietta's directions to park in an unlit section of street near her house that I realized he wasn't warning me to be prepared for inclement weather.

While guiding me to this desolate spot, she'd casually been running her hand up and down the inside of my thigh. I knew it was more than a chance connection, but in my naivete, I assumed her moves had a purpose, specifically to help with the directions. Down the leg meant turn right, up the leg, left. It wasn't until she began touching something far more sensitive that I realized I'd been deceived. A few long kisses with her tongue exploring my mouth and I knew the score. It was me.

Now, I don't want to infer her actions offended me, nor did I ever consider whether they were morally right or wrong. On the contrary, when she took my hand and brought it to her bare breast, I thought the whole experience was, well...invigorating. The same was true when she guided my hand on a journey up the inside of her skirt, over her hose to her garter belt. That's when I realized I had the beginnings of a boner.

What happened next extended the rules of engagement for youthful skirmishing during that era. She slipped out the door opening, climbed into the rear of the car and plopped onto the mattresses. Before I was fully attuned to what she expected to happen, Henrietta implored me to action with a great Marilyn Monroe impersonation. In a husky voice she murmured, "Come and get it while it's hot!"

Unfortunately, during my rush to escape from the vehicle, I banged my head on the door opening. While a knock like that would have been easy to ignore under other circumstances, at that particular moment, I was blind-sided by a series of lurid visions. Although I tried to will them away, my brain became fixated on every movie about venereal diseases I'd ever been exposed to in health class. Moreover, I began to hear voices. There was old man Hopkins, the health teacher, who once said, "Better to have callouses on your palms than pustules on your penis." Then, I was facing my mother over the kitchen table as she was saying, "Bad girls want to trap a nice boy like you into giving them a baby." And then, if that wasn't enough advice to spoil the experience, I remembered hearing Mrs. Clifford next door yelling out an upstairs window, "Donnn't dooo it!" as her oldest daughter, Patricia, was about to ride off with her boyfriend.

I also heard another voice, this one more direct and insistent. "Come on," Henrietta was saying. "We haven't got all night." However, by then I was feeling a little squeamish, because I didn't exactly know how to go about making Henrietta happy. I also was obsessed with a greater issue. What if we messed up Gibby's mattress in some way. Wasn't I honor bound to return the car in the same pristine condition in which it was given?

"Are you coming or not?" she yelled.

"I guess I'm not," I replied.

Little did I suspect my answer would send her into spasms of uncontrollable tears. I had always believed hot girls never cried, and health class never addressed that subject.

"I'm sorry," I offered when she finally stopped blubbering. "Let me drive you home."

"Alright," she said in a wee, little-girl voice complete with a few delayed sobs.

At that moment with my manhood deflated, my feelings for Henrietta Herdklotz turned to tenderness. I continued to embrace those warm feelings as the brisk air blew through the door openings on the short ride back to her house.

I parked at the curb. Wanting to end the evening on a better note, I reached out to her with my right hand. But my offering was too little and too late for Henrietta. She had already slipped out the opening and was standing on the sidewalk. That's when she indignantly proclaimed, "The last time I was in the back seat of this car, I was with a real man!"

At that moment, she might as well have pulled a pistol from her purse and shot me, or if I had one I might have used it on Gibby when I returned the car. Instead, by the time I reached Gibby's house and he dropped me off at home, my passion for murder had cooled. Plus, I'd made a new plan. If the time was ever right, I might share my feelings about the incident with my dad.

The episode opened my eyes to the exciting possibilities other guys talked about in the locker room. However, I felt betrayed by

Gibby and Henrietta Herdklotz doing it on the mattresses in the back of his Dream Machine while I never had a clue.

As it turned out, I never did have a discussion about sex with my dad. The whole topic wreaked of embarrassment for me and perhaps would have for him as well. It wasn't that Mike O'Malley was a prude or a saint. I'd heard some of the jokes he'd told, and blue words cascaded from his mouth like Niagara Falls. However, discussing intimacy was not something I'd expect him to be comfortable with, and I wasn't about to test him.

In October, following the Henrietta Happening, my grandparents left their home in Michigan to visit us in Rockford for a week or so. I had just arrived home from high school and found Grandpa O'Malley dozing on the couch in the living room. My dad was at work and my mother and grandmother were shopping. After slamming the closet door, I managed to make enough noise to wake him and bring him to his feet.

"No homework?" he asked standing before me eye-to-eye.

Although I'd just dumped the pile of books I was supposed to study on the kitchen table, I answered, "Just a little. I'll do it tonight. Do you want to play cribbage?"

He yawned and stretched. "I suppose I can whip you a few games before I get too bored."

We were part way through the game, and I was way, way behind when I said, "Can I ask you something, Grandpa?"

"Sure, just as long as I don't have to throw in this game. I think I got you skunked."

After agreeing to continue, I proceeded to tell him the whole story of Henrietta Herdklotz. He listened with a bland expression on his face. When I finished, I looked at him tentatively, then asked, "Did I do the right thing?"

After thinking for a second, he groaned and said, "Yeah. For all the wrong reasons. Better to do the right thing for the right reason."

I'm sure I looked perplexed, because he began to clarify his point. "Tim, you knew what kind of a girl she was before your date, didn't you?"

"Well...not exactly. I'd heard a few things ..."

"With women, where there's smoke there's usually fire. I know and you know you were tryin' on some new clothes with this girl to see whether they fit you. As it turned out, they were a little snug around the collar, and you got out of there. That was good, but you should never have gone out with a girl like that in the first place."

"But other guys do it."

"Sure they do. If that weren't so, all girls would be virgins when they put on the bridal veil, and there wouldn't be any VD or illegitimate kids. Personally, I'd prefer my grandson just share the beauty of sex with a woman he loves and who loves him." He stared at me a second so the wisdom of his words could sink in. Then he grossed me out with his final comment. Having casual sex with any old girl is like taking a dump. You certainly don't have anything beautiful to look back on when you're done."

I didn't know whether to laugh or to be horrified that the grandfather I respected would say such a thing to his sixteen-year-old grandson, but I have to admit I understood the analogy. What he said next was also clear. "Tim, if you repeat what I just said to anyone, I'm taking you out of my will and giving your share to the Little Sisters of the Poor."

I laughed. "I promise, Grandpa."

He smiled and handed me the deck of cards. "Good, now shut up and play this hand."

Later, after he did skunk me, and we were starting a new game, he said with a grin, "Tim, I'm glad you felt comfortable asking your old grandfather about such things. I only wish I had better answers for your tough questions. Loving one woman and being true to her limited my desire to research a very complicated subject."

I'm sure my father had the same limited experience with women as my grandpa, but knowing him, I'm sure the answers I was looking for wouldn't have come so freely. He once told me that according to my grandfather, the reason he was an only child had nothing to do with any difficulty grandpa had getting my grandmother pregnant again and everything to do with my father's breech birth. Apparently my grandmother about died in the process of the midwife getting him turned around so he'd come out head first. Plus, he said, your grandmother was in such pain she was praying for her own death. After that experience, both my grandparents agreed one pregnancy like that was enough.

He began to chuckle. "You know, Tim, although I was never told how they avoided another pregnancy, I heard enough strange noises through the walls to know they weren't relying on abstinence to accomplish their goal."

My dad was still chuckling when I said, "The next time I see Grandpa O'Malley at the nursing home, I'll ask him and report back to you. He's never been shy about talking sex with me."

"You're kidding. When I was young, he never would talk to me about it."

"Did you ask?"

"Of course not. I wouldn't want him to know I thought about such things."

I grinned. "I never talked to you for the same reason."

My dad frowned. "Thank goodness. I wouldn't have known what to say."

My father once told me that when he was in the contemplation stage of asking Sara, my mother, to marry him, he asked her opinion about having children. "If it was up to me," she said, "I'd have three. Two boys and a girl, just like my mother had. A daughter would help me around the house with chores and cooking, and once she had children of her own, she'd come to me for advice, and we'd go out for coffee and *girl talk*."

"What about the boys?"

"They'd be your buddies, Mike," Sara said. "They'd play sports constantly, and you'd coach them, and they'd try to make you proud. You'd fish and hunt and *ooh* and *ahh* over cars, and at the end of the day they'd come home to eat my cooking, hug me and play me like a fiddle. I'd probably let them get away with anything, just like my brothers did with my mom."

When they did get married, it was the heart of the Depression. Dad held a succession of jobs selling factory supplies to companies that had little use for the products he had to sell. At least he had something to do. My mother couldn't find any job that paid. Still, after ten years they did have me, but my brother and sister never showed up.

One night before Michael left for college, my dad came to our house for dinner after visiting my mother at the nursing home. Two things impressed me. He was quite sober and unusually reflective. Following dinner I sent Michael upstairs ostensibly to do his homework, and my dad began to talk. "Tim, the real irony of our circumstances back when you were little has hit me especially hard since your mother has been slipping away. At the very point in our lives when we had all the time in the world to care for a houseful of children, we were so poor that we tried every method we knew of to keep from having them. Then, by the time we finally had you, Tim, your mother was told by the doctor not to have any more." Dad turned to Claire and said, "True to Sara's plan back then, Tim and I formed a bond that matched her expectations." Then he grinned. "And, for sure, he always had his mother wrapped around his little finger." Suddenly tears glistened his eyes. "I just wish we'd had that little girl for her."

Claire said, "Mike, before and after Marie died, Sara and I drank a lot of coffee together. She helped me with my grief, always listened and gave me great advice. She was a wonderful friend and mother to me."

"I didn't know that," he said. "Thank you for telling me, Claire."

Chapter 26

TIM O'MALLEY

From the time I was a small child, I always viewed Grandpa O'Malley as a god, forcing my father to promote a more reasoned view. At times that meant attempting to tear him down in my eyes. A typical example occurred over the news that Grandpa had a brother, Jacob.

My dad was sharing his newly acquired insight into our family history while we were walking together in the forest preserve on a beautiful June day six years ago. How do I keep track of such mundane facts? Actually, it's easy to pinpoint the date. Marie was still alive and my mother was still functioning well enough to be living at home. Also, Claire and I had just moved into our new house and my grandpa and grandma had just moved from Michigan into my parents' home in Rockford, and until that day, I never recalled my dad and I ever taking a walk together–nor have we since.

Preceding the revelation by my father, I had often thought it unique that my grandfather, John, my father, Mike, and I were all males with no siblings. Now, well into my thirties, I found out the long-hidden fact from my previously clueless father that my assumption was incorrect. While I was somewhat surprised at the finding, he was overwhelmed by the discovery. Within the first few minutes of our walk he entered into an irrational, eyebrow raising rant toward my grandfather. "How would I know my father had a brother," he fumed. "I'd never met one, he'd never spoken of one and my mother never even hinted such a person existed. It's just like my parents to keep me in the dark about something important like that."

I listened in silence, shocked that he was trembling by the time he got the words out.

"Can you believe your grandpa hadn't seen his brother since he left home at age fifteen?" he said shaking his head. "The morning my father received the call that Jacob O'Malley was dying, I was at work. Wouldn't you think he'd mention it to me?"

Seeing his agitation, I said I thought it strange he hadn't.

"But, no, not your grandfather. Just like a politician burying a dirty secret, he never mentioned the call to me or Sara or anyone except perhaps my mother, Flo, who, of course, wouldn't tell me anyway."

"That doesn't sound like Grandpa O'Malley," I said.

"You don't know him like I do. When he wants to be, he can be one of the most secretive and obstinate men alive."

"So, how did you find out?"

"As it happened, that evening I received a call from Jacob's daughter, a cousin I never knew existed, pleading with me to encourage my father to reunite with his brother while he still could. I explained my astonishment at being left in the dark about her father, but promised I'd try to get him there. Since he hadn't yet had his first stroke, and had the time and the money, there was no excuse for my father not responding by hopping a plane and trying to see Jacob. In the end, he agreed to go, but not until he put up a big fuss."

"Was he glad he went?" I asked.

"How would I know! He flew down to Arkansas. His brother died. He flew home. And, he's never said a word about it since. I've given up asking."

"Maybe I'll ask him sometime," I said.

"You do so at your own risk. I'll never confront him about it again."

I did bring up the subject once several years later while I was driving my grandfather to the grocery store after he was living on his own in an apartment in Rockford. "I understand you had a brother," I said casually.

I could feel his eyes boring holes in the side of my face. "So, your dad told you?"

"Yes, a long time ago."

"Then, you already know about Jacob?"

"Yes"

"Then, why bring it up?"

I picked up on his pique. "That's a good question. Curiosity, I guess."

He was silent on the subject for the rest of the trip to the store and all during the time we were filling his cart. As I was driving him back to his apartment, he said out of the blue, "There are two lessons to be learned, Tim."

"Lessons?" I'd truly forgotten my earlier inquiry. "What are you talking about, Grandpa?"

"My brother, Jacob. The first lesson is for you. If you are basing your opinions on hearsay, don't be too quick to condemn."

"I wasn't condemning. I just wanted to know more about a long lost relative of mine."

"Your father is pissed with me, but he'll never know the entire story. Nor will you. So, what right does he or you have to form an opinion about my relationship with my brother."

I sighed. "I'm sorry I brought it up. I'll never mention it again."

"Good," he said and then remained silent as I carried his two bags of groceries into his ground floor apartment and began putting them in their proper place in his fridge and cupboards.

As I was placing the last can on the shelf, he suddenly broke his silence. "I said there were two lessons. It took me a long time to learn the second one." He reached over and touched my arm. "I always idolized my older brother, but he told my father a bunch of lies about me when we were kids that turned my father against me and drove me from home. I should have confronted Jacob then and there instead of running away and building a wall between us. There isn't much I regret doing in my life, but maintaining that wall between Jacob and me was a mistake."

"And, you resent your son bringing it up?"

"I don't really resent anything Mike thinks or feels. I just want to avoid suffering any more consequences from my own self-inflicted stupidity."

I hugged him and started for the door to the hall when he reached out and grabbed my arm. "I guess there is another lesson you should take to heart, Tim." I turned toward him and saw him smile. Then he said, "In the long run, it's always better to forgive than drive a wedge between you and someone who might have played a part in your life. Maybe we both could have found redemption."

Chapter 27

MIKE O'MALLEY

I stopped by the nursing home to visit Sara this afternoon, but the nurse wouldn't let me see her. They think she has pneumonia, although it could just be a bad cough and cold. Since Sara can't describe her symptoms, they're just guessing. They are also isolating her from the other residents and outsiders, like me. So instead of spending the time with her, I visited my dad.

When I arrived, he and Annabelle were working on his *words*, so I sat down and listened until they took a break. That Annabelle is something. So patient and kind. I can see why dad just loves her. Anyway, watching them work reminded me of another sandhog family who were close friends of my folks back when I was a young teenager in 1918. The thoughts came in such a rush, I decided to stay and record what I remembered about them.

At the time, Otis and Cora Lundy and their son, Richard, were frequent visitors to our apartment as were Uncle Thomas and Aunt Prudy. We visited their homes as well. Interestingly, the three families never partied together, ostensibly because all three apartments were too small to handle six people at a time. At least, that's what my mother told me. Looking back from my vantage point today, I think there was another reason. It was the early 1920s, and I'm not so sure Uncle Thomas and Aunt Prudy were as comfortable as my folks were entertaining a Negro family in their home.

Mr. Lundy, a tall and wiry mustachioed man with a wide toothy smile, worked with my father. In 1918, he also had the distinction of becoming the first black man to become a foreman on any construction project in Baltimore. While his coronation was a result of impressing the big bosses with his peaceful nature and skill with explosives, my father embraced him because he was a lot like him, caring and likeable on the outside, tough as nails on the inside, and they always kept their word. Since they were like two peas in a pod, it was only natural for our families to have a great deal more in common than the social mores of the day might encourage.

Mr. Lundy's wife, Cora, was a graduate of Coppin College, an all-Negro school, and worked as a librarian. She also was the best-educated woman I'd ever met to that point. Sometimes when they visited, she brought me books that she hoped would broaden my knowledge of the various sciences. At other times, she'd bring me biographies of famous leaders, like Washington, Benjamin Franklin and Lincoln, with the hope they would open my eyes to broader ideals and teach me facts I hadn't learned in school. On occasion, she'd even quiz me on what I'd learned. "Michael, why did George Washington lead the Revolution against the British?" Or, "Why did President Lincoln free the slaves, Michael?" Cora Lundy was the only person other than my mother to ever call me Michael, and unlike my mother, she didn't have to be angry at me to do it.

Sometimes we had spelling bees. *We* meant her good-natured son, Richard, and me. Richard was three years older, athletically gifted and far more interested in sports than spelling. To keep the contest competitive in the early stretches, she gave Richard words like *repeat* and *complete*, while I was blessed with *receive* and *believe*. Later when Mrs. Lundy introduced more difficult words, Richard got *rebellion* and *trailblazer*, while I was given *patriarchal* and *misanthrope* to keep the competition more even. No matter. It was fun and challenging, and I never lost sight of the goal which was improving our spelling. I'm not sure Richard ever grasped his mother's intention.

It wasn't all work with Mrs. Lundy, even though she wanted us to exercise our minds a bit more than we were apt to do if left to our own initiative. Sometimes, instead of a test, she would bring a novel for me to read just because she thought I might enjoy it. I always did. Later on in high school I learned that the classic treasures by Dickens, Dumas and Conrad that Mrs. Lundy loaned to me and which I learned to love, had to be force-fed to my fellow students. For once in my life my book reports brought me fame instead of notoriety, and that helped compensate for all the upheaval I endured moving from school to school.

While I have always credited my love of literature to Mrs. Lundy, I learned to love baseball through her son, Richard. He was the one who got me interested in improving my game by invading my complacency with his infectious enthusiasm. Prior to my flu-prevention Portsmouth summer and Richard becoming my first teacher, I was a splinter of a kid content to toss a ball against a brick wall and field the rebound, or swing at a small stone with a severed tree branch. By the time I met Richard, he was a fifteen-year-old sandlot shortstop who already had Negro League scouts drooling over his talent. Just playing catch with him on the sidewalk outside my parents' apartment motivated me to become better. In addition, according to my father's later accounts, it scared the crap out of the all-white neighborhood.

Certainly Richard's appearances didn't improve my social status, either. One time when Billy Simmons was hanging around Richard and me hoping we'd invite him to play three-cornered catch, his mother yelled out the window, "Billy, come in this instant. You haven't done your chores." Or, there was the time Charlie Caswell was playing with us, and he was told to "Come home for dinner." I knew something was fishy. It was only three o'clock.

Aside from teaching me to play baseball and introducing me to bigotry, it was Richard and his black teenaged friends who challenged me to raise the quality of my game. Each time we visited the home his parents owned in West Baltimore, and we slipped out to play ball in the street, my eyes were opened to how good I needed to be. In my neighborhood, I was content to play some scrub baseball with the duds that lived around there. When I was with Richard and his friends, I wanted to be a PLAYER like they were.

Over time, I actually became a very good sandlot second baseman, and by my early twenties I'd evolved into a decent amateur player. However, my skills paled compared to Richard who turned into the finest ballplayer I ever saw. During his prime he was the star shortstop for the Baltimore Black Sox in both the Eastern Colored League and the American Negro League. Although in those days a black ballplayer couldn't play in the major leagues, he was as good as any of them and my all-time hero.

I eventually gave up playing baseball in my late twenties. The country was deep into the Depression, Sara was pregnant with Tim, and I needed to work as many jobs as I could find that would pay the rent and help feed the family. However, I continued to enjoy it as a spectator and fan. Later on, it was Tim who succeeded at the game. He was a good enough pitcher to be offered a minor league contract with the LA Dodgers, but he chickened out and turned it down to marry his college sweetheart, Claire. The present PLAYER in the O'Malley family is my grandson, Michael. He is a terrific college pitcher, and I'm rooting for him to continue to develop so he can sign one of those whopping thirty-or forty-thousand dollar major league contracts they offer these days to kids with potential.

My father, John O'Malley, had a special gift, too. He could turn a thoughtful act of kindness into an enduring friendship that many times allowed him to turn the key and enter an exclusive world that would not ordinarily be open to a working man like himself. I can remember us cleaning the day's catch for a commercial fisherman so the man would take us out on his boat. He'd help farmers cut down trees for some firewood or for the right to hunt on his land. He'd lend small sums of money without a hope of repayment, only to be rewarded in some tangible way for years to come. Whether the recipient of his generosity was rich or poor, whatever gift was bestowed always found a way back to him.

His gift to Otis Lundy was a perfect example. He gave him his first meaningful job, fought the bosses to have him promoted to foreman and gave him a shotgun to hunt with on land that never had been open to a Negro hunter. Moreover, my father was totally oblivious to what he or his family might lose because of our friendship with the Lundys.

While I'm here and Annabelle takes Dad to PT, I'm going to get all these Lundy memories on the machine.

One of the sandhogs, Peter O'Leary, was a big guy even for an Irishman, and short-tempered to the point where without Boomer's advocacy, my dad would never have hired him as a member of the crew to work underground on a job as delicate as the excavation for the Port Authority Building in Baltimore. Unlike most of the jobs where the crews would blast through bedrock to pour the pilings that anchored the structure, the PA building, as it was called, was built on reclaimed land at the water's edge. Even the most veteran Irish sandhog was edgy working in an environment where a sudden gusher could fill the excavation with sea water and drown them before anyone on top could institute a rescue. Knowing this, and sensing the fears the less experienced Negro workers were feeling, my father, Otis and Boomer took special pains to closely supervise each worker's activity to insure against some small mistake in judgment or deed doing in the whole crew.

Besides attempting to avoid errors, my father reasoned that the less time spent on the PA job the better for everyone involved. So he took it upon himself to push all of the men to increase their output. While none of the men enjoyed responding to added pressure, Peter O'Leary was especially rankled by my father's prodding.

One morning when Boomer was working in another cell of the excavation away from the temperamental O'Leary, the big man became pissed off. "Get off my goddamn back, John O'Malley," he yelled. "I know what I'm doin,' and I know how long it takes." He nodded over his shoulder at Otis Lundy who was within earshot, and said, "If you'd use your mouth on the darky over there instead of me and the boys, maybe his coons would work harder, and we'd all be out of this hellhole sooner."

According to what some nearby hogs told my Uncle Thomas, my dad didn't say a word as he turned and began walking away. Then, after a few steps he looped back and faced up to O'Leary. Very calmly, he said, "You'll be out sooner than most, Peter O'Leary. When the day's over, collect your pay because you're not coming back."

With that the angry man went berserk, waving his arms and yelling at his Irish mates. "John O'Malley just sacked me. If he can do that to his best sandhog, just think what he could do to you. You better get the bastard before he gets you."

Apparently, to a man, each returned to his work as if nothing out of the ordinary had happened. Not only that, my father further fueled his rage by turning his back on him once again and calmly walking away. After striking out in his plea for support from his countrymen and then seeing his tormentor walk away, O'Leary blew a gasket. He raced after my father and slammed his shovel onto the back of his head and watched him crumple to the floor of the excavation. Then, standing over him with his shovel poised for another strike, he waited to see if my father would try to move. When he eventually did rise to his hands and knees, O'Leary drove him back to the gravel floor with a strike to his back.

What O'Leary didn't see was Otis Lundy flying at him shoulder first. The blow knocked him to the ground, and seconds later he lay on his back with the smaller black man's forearm bearing down on his throat.

By the time my Uncle Thomas was summoned to the scene, a circle of Irishmen encircled Dad. He was sitting up with blood oozing from the back of his head and through the back of his shirt.

His attacker continued to be held down by Otis Lundy. What was amazing was no one in the circle made the slightest move to free O'Leary from the black man's grasp. Only when dad said, "Get him out of here, Boomer," did Uncle Thomas conscript two workers to free him from Otis Lundy's grasp and help escort the now mute and subdued offender up to ground level on the hoist and send him home on a streetcar with the warning, "Don't ever come back."

While they were gone, Otis Lundy summoned one of his men and told him to fetch the first aid kit. Then, after helping my dad struggle to his feet and shed his bloodstained shirt, he applied iodine to his cuts. Later, working the rest of the day bare to the waist, my father exhorted his men to "make up for lost time" so he could "go home happy." What he didn't say, Uncle Thomas said for him. "That Scotsman is damn lucky to have a friend like Otis Lundy."

Whenever I think of Otis Lundy and his family, I give thanks to Cora Lundy for my love of good literature, I pay homage to Richard for imbedding the game of baseball into the hearts and psyches of three generations of O'Malleys and most of all, I pray for Mr. Lundy's eternal soul because of what he did for my father that day down in the hole.

Chapter 28

TIM O'MALLEY

What a strange Saturday morning! I woke up early and put in an hour or so of work on grandpa's stories. What I typed wasn't anything insightful, just some sketchy narrative about his work in New York and Chicago. According to what he recorded, Grandpa O'Malley worked on an art deco building in New York that became the tallest building in the world until the Empire State Building was completed. I have to check out the Encyclopedia Britannica for the building's name, because grandpa was a little vague about it. He was proud, though, just like he was about working on the Palmolive Building in downtown Chicago several years later when he and grandma lived in Calumet City, Indiana.

Later in the day, I stopped over at Dad's house to return the hand cultivator I'd borrowed the previous weekend. I decided to ask him about grandpa's recollection. He was equally vague about the building in New York, but when I brought up the Palmolive Building, he snorted. "You mean the Playboy Building don't you, Tim?"

I tossed him a quizzical look because I had no idea what he was talking about.

He laughed. "When Hugh Hefner bought the building a few years ago, he changed the name. Now it's a bunny hutch." Continuing to grin, he added, "I wonder if your grandfather would still be as proud of his work if he knew Playboy was headquartered there now. God only knows what my mother would be thinking if she were alive."

"I doubt Grandpa would be too upset."

"Don't be so sure, Tim. When it came to women, your grandfather was as square as they came. He was as true to his Flo as any man could be to his wife. While a lot of the "boys" were philanderers, I'd bet a thousand dollars he never even thought of straying."

"I guess it's in the genes," I said, leaving dad a little wiggle room for a confession if he wanted to clear up any misconceptions I might be carrying.

He grinned. "It's definitely in my genes, Mr. Smarty Pants. I may drink, but I always know when to go home to my wife."

Suddenly, he began to cry. With tears streaming down his cheeks, he reached into his pants pocket and took out a handkerchief. "It's so hard, Tim. It's so, so hard."

I nodded.

Dabbing at his tears he said, "I'm so sorry, Tim. Of all people you certainly know how hard it is to lose someone you love."

I reached out to him and he threw his arms around me, and we hugged and cried together, probably for the first time ever.

Later, sitting across from Claire at the dinner table, I told her about the incident. She listened quietly, then stood up and walked around the table and kissed me gently on the cheek. "Good for you guys," she whispered. "Good for you."

That night our lovemaking reached a depth we hadn't experienced since Marie died.

Afterward, remembering Dad's tears, I wondered if he visited my mother and went to the bar as usual. Still, judging from his mood when I left him, he may have stayed home to begin thinking about a new life for himself. I hope it was the latter.

Chapter 29

MIKE O'MALLEY

I'm sorry for so many things I doubt I can list them all in this one recording in my father's room at Highland Manor. This will not be one of those classic 'Forgive me Father, for I have sinned' confessions because I'm not Catholic and Annabelle has been kind enough to wheel Dad down to dinner so I can be alone with my thoughts. However, I'm well aware that Tim will be reading them and hopefully he will edit them kindly before the final version of our family memoir is set to rest.

First, a note to Tim. "Thank you for the hug the other night and thank you for making the effort to record the meaningful events and relationships in my father's and my life. In addition, thank you for letting me participate in this vehicle. My involvement has given me a better understanding of my distant past, and reliving incidents from it have helped me deal with my present. Finally, it has allowed me to understand, know and love each of you for who you are rather than who I thought I wanted you to be.

"Now for the apologies. When I decided my mother and father should move to Rockford and live with us, I didn't realize Sara was beginning her descent into dementia. At the time I just assumed her forgetfulness and inability to recall names and events from the past were the normal symptoms of aging. It wasn't until my parents had been living with us for six or eight months that Sara's lapses became more frequent and at times bizarre; like climbing out the living room window. When I asked her why she did it, she answered, 'Because you moved the front door.'

"As the number of events increased, I felt compelled to find a cause, and all I could come up with was one thing. Since my mother and Sara were never simpatico, I feared the stress of mom's constant presence was driving her batty. After all, living with my parents was driving me crazy, and I wasn't even with them all day like Sara was. Then my mother died, and my father had a stroke, and Sara kept getting worse. That cemented the reality of her dementia, and I've been sorry ever since for not believing it sooner.

"At sixty-seven I've finally come to realize I've spent much of my adult life needlessly bitching about my father's job. While it was disruptive to my schooling to move all the time, I would never have known an Uncle Thomas and Aunt Prudy in Baltimore, or enjoyed summers in Maine with Grandpa and Grandma Ferland. I certainly wouldn't have had a wonderful teacher like Cora Lundy to expose me to classic literature or her son, Richard, to introduce me to baseball. Had we not moved to Calumet City, Indiana, or New York City or Cleveland, I would have missed countless opportunities to broaden my experiences and develop an interest in geography. Most important of all, if my parents hadn't moved to East St. Louis, I would never have met and married Sara, had Tim and forty-three years of happiness. I'm sorry for bitching, Dad. I should have been thanking you."

Chapter 30

DIARY OF A SANDHOG

Sean O'Donnell wasn't a bad egg. It was just that he was like an odd sized package going through the mail. He needed special handling. True, Boomer and I had grown tired of his habit of showing up at work twice a month so soused to the gills he could barely walk. But, when he was sober, he worked hard and smart, was always friendly with everyone and did have the financial burden of keeping six small bellies filled at home. So, I gave him some slack. When he wasn't sober enough to work in the hole, instead of firing him, I'd personally walk him to the street car, wait with him to make sure he caught the right tram home and pray he'd know when to get off.

To his credit, on the next day following one of his "sick days," Sean always beat me to work and sheepishly apologized for causing me "trouble" the day before. Then, he'd work like the devil on roller skates attempting to do the work of two men to impress me and atone for his error in judgment.

While an Irish lad missing work because he was soused was never a rarity, for several reasons Sean's misadventures threw the whole crew into turmoil. He was the un-official leader of the crew that removed the debris from the floor of the tunnel after the dynamite blast had broken loose a wall of solid rock, and when he was missing, the remainder of the crew worked at half speed. This both frustrated me and made the big bosses question my leadership. However, there was a second more insidious reason. He was the leader of an integrated crew. Had he been a common hand or had his crew been made up entirely of Irish boys, no one would have batted an eye, because missing work for overstepping his pint limit was quite common and always forgivable. In fact, on some all-Irish crews, working through a hangover earned the mate a mite more respect than working sober. On those crews the standard treatment would be to laud, praise and tease him, because all had traveled his road at one time or another. It was also a sign of respect for coming to work and a signal his behavior was totally acceptable.

On our integrated crew, a drunk scene was an affront to the black workers and sometimes a call to war. In my role as the captain, I had one essential job over and above getting the work done. I had to keep my men working together.

Following the Great War, I had put together a solid hardworking crew of Negro workers to work alongside the Irish boys. By tradition and a need for income, these men would never think to miss a day of work unless they were on their deathbed. Also, before Otis Lundy and I became their bosses, sleeping off a drinking spree would have had them fired, or worse ostracized by their friends and family for making it harder for all Negroes. So, my appearing to overlook Sean's periodic indiscretions was an affront to their work ethic.

With Otis taking the lead, we went about convincing the black workers that Sean or any Irishman was never paid on the days he was sent home drunk. After convincing most of the men of this truth, we began another campaign to eradicate past practices. We made sure every black worker understood that if he was sick or injured he should stay home until he was well and his job would be waiting for him.

Once all these new practices were fully in place and accepted, I began to focus on a far different aspect of missing work that had nothing to do with ethnic differences. All too often, I'd observed many workers showing up sick because they didn't want to miss a paycheck and then passing their disease on to other healthy crew members. This was especially true during the influenza outbreak in 1918 when thousands of people died and millions were incapacitated. At one point my crew of forty was cut to fifteen due to the "flu."

After falling behind schedule and discussing the situation with my bosses, we came up with a revolutionary plan. Any worker who had worked for the company for six months could bring a note from a doctor saying he was sick or injured and be paid up to seven days without coming to work. We called it insurance, and it became very popular in the construction industry in the years that followed.

While today we call alcoholism a disease, you better believe that boys like Sean were never paid a dime when they were hung over and that cured a lot of drinking problems.

Chapter 31

MIKE O'MALLEY

On the morning they called me at work to tell me Sara had died, I immediately phoned Tim and then left to visit Fitzgerald's Funeral Home and begin making arrangements. From there I went to Highland Manor to break the news to my father. As had been his habit in recent months, when I rapped on the door, he hollered, "Come in."

By the time I had opened the door and crossed the room to where I was recognizable to him, he was on his feet in front of his chair. "What's the matter?" he asked.

"Sara died," I said moving closer.

"I'm so sorry." Suddenly I was caught in a bear hug. "I loved Sara," he said.

His holding me and the shock of her death finally unleashed my tears. "So did I, Dad. So did I."

For the next few minutes we were silent. While I attempted to recover my composure, my father slowly returned to his arm chair. Feeling an overwhelming need to be near him, I carried the small desk chair we used when we talked into the recorder and placed it next to him. Although I wasn't sure he'd understand my need or be able to fulfill it, I hoped for a large dose of love and compassion. In the preceding fifty years I would have surely felt embarrassed by my next move, but I reached over and let my fingers search out his gnarled hand. In the silence that followed we

173

simply sat hand in hand as the minutes ticked away. His healing touch helped ease my pain and replaced it with a sense of calm. "You're a good man," was all he said.

I needed nothing more.

Later, when I began discussing the funeral arrangements with him, I soon realized we had some things to settle. I had planned on Claire picking him up and bringing him to the church for the service, while Tim and I hosted the visitation. He had other thoughts. "Claire should stand with her husband," he said. "And, Michael, too. He's her only grandson. I just go to the funeral."

Considering his age and the length of time involved, his logic made sense to me. But, if Claire was already there, who was left to take him? I was considering a cab or an employee of the funeral home when he blurted out, "Annabelle, take me. She's family, too."

I started to laugh, but caught myself before I let it out. There was no point in picking a fight over a meaningless technicality. In his mind, Annabelle was family, and judging by what she had done for him over the last year, I'd never argue against it. "Will she be able to drive you to the funeral home?"

"Schoor. The day is Thursday?"

"Yes, at eleven."

"Annabelle and I will be there." He laughed. "Good food?" He waved his hand indicating his current surroundings. "Better than here?"

"We're going to a nice restaurant afterwards." I laughed. "Yes, the food will probably be better than Highland Manor."

"Not shit food?"

"Not shit, Dad."

"Good, Annabelle will be my date. She's family, too."

"I know Dad, and we'll be happy to have her with us."

Chapter 32

TIM O'MALLEY

We got through the day all right yesterday. My father did especially well. I guess mourning my mother's demise on a daily basis over four years as her brain deteriorated had prepared him for the final act. Unlike my father, Claire and I were both shaken. The service brought back all of the painful feelings we shared following our little Marie's death. I suppose, like Grandpa O'Malley, a day will come when we will find relief from our suffering and accept death as part of living. Yet, judging by the feelings of desolation and sorrow that still grip my heart, if that day ever does come, I'm sure it will be a long way off.

Today, when I stopped by Highland Manor to pick up Grandpa's latest cassette, Alice was making his bed. I hadn't seen her for awhile so I was a bit taken back by her sinister grin and hollow "hi." I returned her salutation as I walked past her to greet my grandfather who was sitting in his chair near the window facing my approach. When he recognized me, he clearly said, "Good morning, Tim."

I could tell at once there was no joy in his voice. Bending down, I hugged him and asked, "What's wrong, Grandpa?"

To my surprise, he nodded toward Alice. Turning quickly, I caught her in mid-stare, watching and listening to our conversation.

"Annabelle's gone," he said.

Now, I've observed my grandfather exercise his own unique one-word vocabulary countless times to express a multitude of emotions, but this morning there was no mistaking his mood or the intended recipient of his "Shit! Shit! Shit!" Alice was right there silently going about her labors. When I reached out to him to calm him, he was shaking. I realized he was as angry as I'd ever seen him.

"Annabelle's gone," he repeated. "Shit!"

"What do you mean, gone?" I asked. Then I turned to Alice who was inching out of the room and addressed the question to her.

She seemed eager to answer. "Yesterday, the administration found out that woman drove Mr. O'Malley in her car. It's against the rules to take a resident away from the premises without obtaining permission."

"You mean she was terminated because no one in our grieving family remembered to ask permission for Annabelle to help us out? That's terrible. Annabelle is such a nice woman. I'm surprised that under the circumstances, they wouldn't overlook it."

"That Negress always got special treatment. She certainly wasn't treated like the rest of the staff."

"But, my father asked her to drive my grandfather to my mother's funeral. We pay for his care. She was doing us a favor."

"That won't save her this time."

"I can't believe it. How would they even know?"

"She should have tried to get permission," Alice said.

"So you squealed on her?"

She shrugged, "Maybe a little birdie told them!" Snarling, she added, "All I know is yesterday she got what was coming to her. Good riddance, I'd say."

Suddenly, Grandpa O'Malley picked up his cane from the floor, stood up and began waving it wildly as Alice backed towards the door. I didn't try to stop him because I knew he couldn't get close enough to hit her unless I held her back which was an option I was considering. Instead, I let her escape to the corridor followed by a chorus of "bitch, shit, bitches." In my heart I sang tenor and felt damn good about it.

Once I had Grandpa settled into his chair, and we had a chance to talk about Annabelle, I realized just how much they cared about each other. She'd do anything for him, and that was her downfall. She must have known she'd get in trouble for driving him to the funeral, but she was more concerned they'd turn her down and disappoint him and us. So, she took the chance and got caught. Now it was up to us to support my grandfather by going to the office and pleading her case.

Ten minutes later, I was granted a hearing in front of the imperious female Director of Resident Services, in other words, the boss. I pleaded Annabelle's case and was told there had been so many complaints from the floor staff over the last year, she couldn't rescind her decision to terminate Mrs. Jackson. I left the office mumbling grandpa's phrase, "shitbitch."

Chapter 33

MIKE O'MALLEY

That evening after Tim explained Annabelle's dismissal to me, I vented my feelings in a way that would have made my father proud. Since we were partly to blame for her firing because we didn't check into the procedures, Tim and I were in total agreement that the O'Malleys had to do something about it. My son, Tim, has always been a good idea man, so I wasn't surprised when he already had a plan in mind before he called me. Once I bought into it, I followed through with my father. By nature, my skills lay more in sales and implementation, so once my father was on board, it was my turn to make the next move.

I called Annabelle.

"When Mr. Tim told me about his wife taking Mr. O'Malley to the funeral, it only seemed right that I drive him so she could be with her husband and you. Even though I knew the rules, I wanted to do it. So Mr. Mike, you just never mind about me. I'll get another job somewhere."

"Be that as it may, Annabelle, we want to show our gratitude for all you've done for my father. So, we'd be pleased if you would bring your husband and children to my son's house for dinner Saturday night as a small thank you."

"Why I declare, that is very thoughtful."

"Will you come?"

"I don't see no reason why we can't. I don't like cooking every day any more than any woman."

"Really! I'm sorry to hear that."

"I don't catch your meaning, Mr. Mike."

"You will after Saturday night."

On Saturday night we charcoal grilled T-bones on the patio for the adults and hamburgers for Annabelle's two boys and served them with a variety of salads Claire had prepared along with potato chips and ice cream sundaes. Along the way, the men downed a few beers and the women and kids drank glasses of lemonade.

As the evening progressed, I was taken by Annabelle's husband, Clem Jackson's, resemblance to my memories of Otis Lundy and his infectious laugh. As it turned out he made his living as a foreman for a manufacturing plant that made parts for cars. Clem was a large, strong-appearing man who, had he been living and working a half century earlier, might have been a sandhog, and had dad been able to speak better, they just might have found they had a lot in common.

Following dinner, Claire and Annabelle cleared the table and the Jackson boys ran off to the den to watch TV. When the adults were back in their places at the table enjoying a cup of coffee, I took the conversation in a new direction and began making my pitch.

"Annabelle, we know we were the cause of your losing your job at Highland Manor, but the real loser isn't here in this room. He's still at that place mourning the loss of the one woman whose friendship meant the most to him."

I watched Annabelle squirm and glance at Clem before I continued. "Because we can't stand the thought of his spending his final years without your TLC, we want you to be with him all the way to the end as his personal caregiver. You can arrange your hours around your family's schedule, and we'll pay you what you were earning at Highland Manor."

She again looked at her husband, but this time she had tears in her eyes. "You all are so wonderful. I just don't know what to say."

"Then, you'll do it?"

"I can't."

Clem spoke for her. "Just this morning she accepted a job at The Woods Nursing Center. She starts on Monday night." Then he added, "Do you realize how lucky she is? Companies just don't hire a Negro woman without checking references from her prior employers. They just experienced an abrupt loss of staff and are very short-handed."

"But, I would have loved to work for you and care for Mr. O'Malley," Annabelle said, dabbing at her eyes with a hankie. "I'm so sorry."

I was stunned. "So be it, then."

Tim's lone voice broke through the hush that followed. "Did I understand you will be working nights, Annabelle?"

With downcast eyes, she said, "That's right, Mr. Tim. But, they promised I will have first crack at any day job that turns up."

"And, you believed them?"

"I wanted to."

"You know, of course, in the meantime you'll never see Clem or the boys because you will be in a different world from them."

I couldn't have been prouder of my son than I was at that moment. Sometime when my back was turned that boy had developed some impressive sales skills. I smiled to myself. Now that he had Annabelle's and Clem's attention, I wondered how he would close the deal.

"You know," Tim said, "I've spent too much time walled off from my family focusing only on myself and my pain and grief. It's been damaging to all of us. Of course, I know my situation is very different from yours, but the hardship of being separated from those who love you can have unexpected consequences."

I was glad I was listening, because I think a bit of the message was meant for my ears. Still, I wasn't at all sure where Tim was going with it.

"What I'm trying to say is, I think your family will be better off if you accept our offer. You'll only work weekdays, you'll be home for meals and evenings and you can arrange your schedule so you don't have to miss any of your sons' activities."

I could see she was tempted, but turning down a job offer in her field was dangerous. If the word got out, she might never get work. Tim must have sensed her reluctance, so he took a different tact. Pretending I wasn't there, he moved closer to Annabelle and lowered his voice and turned confidential. "Although my grandfather loves and needs you, my father needs you, too. While he's been on his own, he's proven he's not a decent cook or much of a housekeeper. He really needs someone with your skills." Smiling, he added, "He is capable of buying his own groceries if you were to give him a list."

Before I could manufacture a futile protest, especially because I knew he was right, Tim said, I'll add $3.00 an hour to the wages my father pays you to take that responsibility off of Claire." I want her to do all those things for me. After all, I'm an O'Malley, too."

Clem began laughing. Turning to her, he said, "The man pleads a case too strong to refuse, sweetheart. Take the job."

I stood up and shook Clem's hand and asked permission to hug Annabelle. Later, after they all left, I gave Tim a bear hug, kissed him on the cheek and went home happy.

The next day I drove to Highland Manor and filled my father in on the plan. "Within the week," I told him, "You'll be back in your old bedroom at my house and Annabelle will be there to help you." I thought the tough old sandhog was going to cry, he was so happy.

On Friday, as I was about to wheel him down the hall toward the front entrance for the last time, Alice strolled by. My father must have caught a glimpse of her because she didn't say anything to identify herself to him. "Shit, bitch," he said just loud enough for her to hear.

I hope she did.

My father had another stroke eighteen months after Annabelle came to care for us. This time he passed quickly from Annabelle's tender loving arms to those of his beloved Flo. On the strength of my recommendation, Annabelle found a day job at another nursing home.

During the past two years, I dated Sara's lifelong friend, Nina. We had all been close friends for many, many years. In fact, I met both Sara and Nina on a double date with my friend, Albert, when my folks lived in East St. Louis in 1927. Nina had been a pilot back in the late 1920's and set a women's altitude record on one of her flights. She was also an artist, and after Sara died, we took several trips to places like Ireland and Italy so she could pursue her interest in watercolor.

In March of 1978 Nina and I were married, and we moved to St. Louis where she had been living. Looking back at both of my successful marriages, I'm thankful that at least one of my parents' many moves paid off for me.

Telling stories into the microphone of Tim's recorder wasn't always a joyous task. Sometimes, like in the case of my "Uncle," Thomas McHale, I had to recall some sad memories that had been lingering beneath the surface of my psyche for years. The fact is Boomer died in 1932 at age 53. He was one of five sandhogs buried alive in a massive cave-in while digging a railroad tunnel through the mountains of Virginia.

He and Aunt Prudy did have one child, a son, Andrew, who was only nine when his father died. Today, he is married, has three boys and is a partner in a Nashville, Tennessee law firm. The last time I connected with him, he said his mother, who was now in her seventies, was living on her own in a suburb of Nashville, clinging to her husband's memory and doting on her three grandsons.

This spring, my grandson, Michael, graduated from college and is working as an actuary in a large insurance company in Boston. He's quite a brilliant young man if I do say so, and his fiancee, Barbara, seems like the perfect balance to his serious nature and workaholic ways with her ready laugh, bright smile and social nature. If it's true that opposites attract, theirs should be a perfect union when they marry next summer. Actually, I can't wait for the next generation of O'Malleys to take their place on this earth. Like Tim's grandfather, the old sandhog, I'll continually encourage them to seek the right direction so they'll never feel lost.

With professional help, both Tim and Claire have found forgiveness. After struggling these last eight years since Marie died, I'm grateful that they've been able to reunite their hearts. In addition, at the first of the year, Tim, by the consensus of the other principals of his advertising agency, was elected President.

Also, Tim is now a published author. *Dairy of a Sandhog* is his first book. It's unequal parts fiction and family memoir.

ABOUT THE AUTHOR

Raymond L. Paul was born in St. Louis, Missouri, during the heart of the Great Depression. His parents moved to Rockford, Illinois, when Ray was four, and he has been a resident ever since. At Rockford West High School, Ray was a quality student-athlete earning honors as a scholar and as a football and baseball player. After graduation he attended the University of Wisconsin/Madison where he majored in Insurance and Finance. He graduated four years later in 1958 with a Bachelor of Business Administration Degree, an offer to play minor league baseball with the Dodgers and a fiancee.

Immediately following graduation, Ray and his future editor, Jo Marie Moerschel, married, and he began a career with Massachusetts Mutual Life Insurance Company. Fifty-five years later, he is still devoted to Jo Marie and proud of his ongoing relationship with Mass Mutual.

Although Ray's interest in writing fiction began in a college English class, carving out a successful career in the financial services industry and being a dedicated father to three daughters precluded any serious involvement. His hiatus from fiction writing lasted almost forty years. During that time their older daughters moved away and started families of their own, and he and Jo Marie weathered the crisis of losing their youngest daughter to meningitis.

After a serious analysis of his decaying golf game, Ray wandered into a writing class at Rock Valley Community College searching for a feasible alternative to his life-long passion. There he found inspiration. He enjoyed the writing projects, and the instructor and many of his adult classmates complimented him on his efforts. After taking two additional college writing classes, some university level workshops and joining a friendly critique group of contemporaries, Ray found a new avocation. Today, in addition to his insurance practice and writing, Ray teaches a simi-lar class to the one he attended at Rock Valley College with the dual hope that he can pay homage to his first teacher and inspire his adult students to become better writers.

Over the past ten years, Ray has written *Cabbage Requiem, Between The Rows,* and *A New Season,* the three novels that make up the George Konert Trilogy. In addition, he has published *Shards,* an eclectic collection of his best short stories, some of which were previously published in various journals and magazines. Two years ago his contemporary novel, *Heaven Lies Between The Foul Lines,* became his fifth book. This story chronicles the life of a young man struggling with the complexities of love, success in the business world and pitching in the major leagues.

His most recent novel, *Annabelle and the Sandhog,* is based on the author's family during the period from the early 1900's to the mid-1970's. Although some of the characters and plot lines in the story surrounding John O'Malley's past and present are fictional, this saga attempts to accurately portray the lives of the tough men and their families who worked underground digging the foundations and pouring the footings for some of the world's tallest buildings.

ALSO BY RAY PAUL

CABBAGE REQUIEM

Even a head of cabbage given as a gift at the right moment can change a life forever. In this poignant and amusing journey of renewal, George Konert proves there is power in the simple things we do for our neighbors and even total strangers. This story carries insight into the heart that never grows old.

BETWEEN THE ROWS

Life seldom turns out the way we design it. We can plan wisely and sow with skill, but how we handle what comes up between the rows defines our character and ultimately our lives. In the second novel of Ray Paul's trilogy about the life of George Konert, his protagonist has settled into a peaceful co-existence with his new wife Catherine. This afterglow lasts until life's inevitable nettles force him into action.

A NEW SEASON

In A NEW SEASON, the final book of the trilogy featuring George Konert, George faces the challenges of his later years with the same biting wit, loving wisdom and dogged determination he displayed in the first two novels. Once again we glimpse George's nurturing spirit as he passionately cares for his family, his friends and his garden with an abiding belief in the future. George is never perfect, and growing older is not always graceful, but we love him for his pluck and determination. The character sticks with you long after you put down the book.

SHARDS

SHARDS is an eclectic collection of short stories. In reality, shards are splinters of colorful glass sprinkled in random patterns. Some are sharp. Others reflect the brilliance of our thoughts. Each piece has the power to entertain, bemuse and /or surprise. While diverse and seemingly unrelated, in this book they become an artful collection of storytelling.

HEAVEN LIES BETWEEN THE FOUL LINES

Todd Mueller grows up in a small town with a father who teaches philosophy at a local college and a mother who handles all the details of his life. Unfortunately for Todd Mueller, their tutelage doesn't provide the skills he needs to cope with a willful young wife nor to survive in a business run by her overbearing and manipulative father. Fortunately for Todd, he acquires two mentors who help him. One is a brilliant but physically challenged inventor who gives Todd perspective, while the other is a tough old park policeman who helps Todd harness the fastball he left behind as a teenager that eventually becomes his ticket to the Major Leagues. Todd's story is about taking wrong turns and still finding one's way.